DEAD QUIET

The house was tomb still. I glanced out the window and listened for the wind or the patter of rain, the sound of crickets or anything at all and heard only a gentle cracking from somewhere downstairs. Then the dog hit the basement doorway and began a frantic barking—only it was more than a bark—it was nearer a roar. He was raging.

The killer was inside the house.

The Missing Moon

Also by Harold Adams

The Man Who Met the Train
The Barbed Wire Noose
The Fourth Widow
The Naked Liar
Paint the Town Red
Murder

Published by
THE MYSTERIOUS PRESS

HAROLD ADAMS
THE MISSING MOON

THE MYSTERIOUS PRESS

New York • London • Tokyo

All characters in this book are fictitious. Any resemblance to actual persons, living or dead, is purely coincidental.

MYSTERIOUS PRESS EDITION

This Mysterious Press Edition is published by arrangement with the author.

Cover design and illustration by Peter Thorpe

Mysterious Press books are published in association with
Warner Books, Inc.
666 Fifth Avenue
New York, N.Y. 10103

A Warner Communications Company

Printed in the United States of America

First Mysterious Press Printing: October, 1988

10   9   8   7   6   5   4   3   2   1

Chapter I

"All I remember," said Boswell, "is I was listening to Miz Bonney and having a few snorts and I got sleepy and the next thing this big fella's shaking me like a terrier with a rat and yelling, 'Why'd you kill her?' Hell, Carl, you know I'd never kill nobody, least of all Miz Bonney."

He should've been scared and upset, but all he showed was sorrow and injured pride in spite of his gray stubble beard, tousled white hair and bloodshot eyes. As usual he wore a stained suit, somewhere between black and gray, wrinkled as pajamas, the universal uniform of the bum. Howie, the young lawyer I'd brought in, stood near the cell door, carefully avoiding contact with anything that'd dirty his seersucker outfit while he watched his client and took shallow breaths to keep the foul air from reaching vital spots in his clean lungs.

"How come you were in her cabin?" I asked. I was sitting on the cell bunk beside Boswell.

"It was the first Saturday night in the month. I always deliver then."

"Did you always go in for a drink when you delivered?"

"No. Mostly I'd just haul in the case, tuck it under

the kitchen sink there, and then she'd pay me and I'd go."

"The police say there was no case in the cabin," said Howie. "There was no liquor in your truck and none on the premises. How do you account for that?"

Boswell shook his head. "Somebody pinched it. I put what I brought in right there under the sink after I took out the one can. There was three gallons in the case and one on the counter that I opened. And I had five more cases in the back of my truck."

"Where'd you park?" I asked.

"Right behind the cabin there, near the door. Them cases is heavy. I don't carry 'em any farther'n I got to."

"The truck was empty," said Howie.

Boswell set his jaw stubbornly. "I had six cases when I got to Miz Bonney's. There's no other reason I'd drive all the way from Corden without I had moon to deliver. I ferget a lot, but I ain't crazy and I wouldn't forget to bring moon."

"What'd she pay you for the case?" asked Howie.

"Jest what she always did: eighteen dollars a gallon, four for seventy dollars. That's two dollars cheaper than most get and ten less a case."

"But you had over three hundred dollars in your wallet. Where'd that come from?"

Boswell scowled at him. "I got other customers, you know."

"You mean you made other deliveries that night?"

"Where else'd I get that much money?"

"Who'd you deliver to?"

Boswell concentrated on the gray cell wall, then shook his head. "I don't recall."

Howie glared at me indignantly and I wished I'd found an older lawyer.

"Okay," I said. "Let's go over what happened, nice and slow. What time did you get to Kate's cabin?"

Boswell frowned, took his stubby pipe from his coat pocket and tamped down the ash he'd let go out when we first came into his cell. He couldn't find matches and I handed over mine.

"It was near sundown," he said. "I remember I had to turn down the rearview mirror cause the light was hitting my eyes."

"A little after eight?"

He nodded and lit the pipe. It smelled a little better than when he burned cigar butts in it.

"You always deliver in the evenings?" asked Howie.

"I don't *always* do nothing."

I explained to Howie that since retiring from the railroad, Boswell had pretty well abandoned time schedules and watches. That didn't exactly horrify Howie; he was more like stunned. He would wear a watch on each wrist and carry a pocket piece to check them against if he weren't afraid people'd think he was odd. He smoothed his glossy black hair with his palm and scowled at the stained concrete floor. Boswell puffed serenely. I rolled a smoke, lit it and asked Boswell to tell us what happened when he got to Kate's.

"Well, I pulled into the backyard there and right away she showed up at the door and held the screen open so's I could carry in the case. I set it on the floor, took one can out and set it on the counter, then shoved the case under the sink. Then she says how about I have a drink to show it's safe and I says why not? And she opened the can, poured out a good belt and we sat down in the living room, by the windows looking out over the lake. The sun was down by then and the water was flatter'n a window pane and had a little pink on it. Everything was just fine—"

"Did you talk?" asked Howie.

"Me? No. *She* talked. Miz Bonney was a great talker."

Howie gave me a dirty look and asked with strained patience what she had talked about.

He shrugged. "It was mostly chatter, you know—"

"Was she nervous or anything?" I asked. "I mean, was it usual for her to offer you a drink?"

"She only done it once before—the first time I came."

"Did you think she was expecting company?"

"Kate always expected company."

Howie twitched and almost stuttered in his irritation. "Well, now. You said she chattered. What did she say?"

Boswell frowned thoughtfully. "She asked me something kind of funny. She asked did I know my daddy."

"What kind of a question's that?" demanded Howie.

"Oh, that's not a bad one. You know the old saying, 'It's a wise man who knows his father.' "

"What'd you say?" I prodded.

"I said no."

"Then what?"

"She asked how come and I said because I'd never seen him and she asked why not, did he die, and I said I didn't know, I just never seen him."

"So what'd she say then?" Boswell's talk was like a frog in a jumping contest: about half the time he wouldn't move without a nudge.

"She asked if I hadn't thought about that and maybe tried to find him."

Howie raised his arms and let them flop against his sides.

"I don't see where this is getting us. Ask him where he made those other deliveries. If we can prove he got paid something like three hundred dollars we can—"

"I'm not asking him that because he won't answer. He's afraid cops'll hassle his customers."

"That's ridiculous. Nobody's going to prosecute illegal liquor purchases for god's sake. Over half the citizens of South Dakota'd be in jail, including most of the police."

Boswell ignored conversation not directed at him and concentrated on relighting his pipe.

"Could be. But he won't take anything for granted," I said. "He won't tell who he sold to if they hang him."

"Well then, this whole case is hopeless."

I leaned toward Boswell as he dropped his dead match in a butt can beside his foot.

"Did she talk about her daddy?" I asked.

Boswell nodded and sucked on his pipe which gurgled, making Howie wince.

"What'd she say?"

"She said she was trying to find him. Since he's been dead for years I figured she shouldn't have any trouble. They buried him out in the Aquatown cemetary and put up a big rock at his head. It ain't likely he's left yet."

"Did you ask her what she meant?"

"She never gave me no chance. She just rambled on till I lost track and as long as she was pouring the moon it didn't seem polite to leave."

"Did she pour a lot?"

"Pretty much," he admitted.

"And finally you fell asleep?"

"Yup. It wasn't polite but I couldn't help it. Just

closed my eyes to rest 'em and the next thing I knew this big fella was shaking me like I was a rat and yelling why'd I do it and I said 'cause I was tired—thinking he meant why'd I gone to sleep. Then he looked in my wallet and wanted to know where I'd got all that money, but he didn't want to listen. He was awful excited and mad. When I saw Miz Bonney there, I could understand. It about made me sick, Carl. How could anything so awful happen with me right by?"

Soon the cell was too much for Howie and he wanted to leave, so we said good-bye to the old man and walked out into the hot sunlight on First Street.

"He's senile," Howie told me. "He's got to be if he expects anybody to believe that story."

"The hell he is. He's old and a little simple, but he doesn't lie, and he knows what's going on except when he's got a snootful and falls asleep. Then he wouldn't hear the last trumpet. And he goddamned well wouldn't kill a spider if it made a web over his mouth. Somebody came in while he was conked out, killed Kate, stole the moon and left him holding the bag."

"And left three hundred dollars in the old man's pocket?"

"Sure. So he'd take the rap. Either that or it didn't occur to him a bum like Boswell'd have a dime in his pocket."

Howie glared up and down the quiet street, blinking against the sunlight. "It doesn't make sense."

"What sense does it make for an old man to kill his best customer and then fall asleep on her couch within spitting distance of the corpse?"

"The police theorize that the strain was too much for him. He killed her, probably after an argument, sat down to get his breath back and passed out from the booze and exertion."

"Theorize my ass. They figure they got a pigeon so why waste time looking for somebody out in the big world when they've got this old bum handy—the bird in hand?"

We walked east along the street, which shimmied under heat waves, and ducked into a café where a tired waitress brought menus and looked sour when we both ordered only coffee. Howie sipped his black and watched as I sugared and creamed mine. His scowl deepened.

"I don't like any of this," he told me. "Not one part. That old man doesn't need a lawyer, he needs a priest."

"Come on, Howie, he's not Catholic and he's not finished. He needs a smart lawyer who won't quit just because he's got a tough case."

"There's nothing tough about this case. It's impossible."

"No, it isn't. I can get you enough character witnesses to fill a hall. There's not a kid that went to school from twenty-four through twenty-eight who won't tell you that old man's a saint."

"Oh, sure, a bootlegger saint. Very convincing."

"Okay, forget it. I'll find a lawyer with guts."

"Guts won't do it. It'll take a miracle."

"I don't think I can hire one."

"You couldn't hire a dishwasher. And that's another sweet part of all this. Who's going to pay me? You going to pass the hat among all those worshipping kids that went to school while Boswell was janitoring at Corden High?"

"Why not. If you're cheap enough to take their dough."

"It's not being cheap to expect pay for professional services, Carl, be reasonable."

We drank coffee and glared at each other for a while.

"All right," he said at last. "Tell me about this woman, Miss Bonney."

"Okay. First, she wasn't a Miss, she was a Mrs., widowed a few years back. Name was Katherine Timmerman before she married. Her old man was Frederick Timmerman the banker who blew his brains out when his bank went bust long before the mess of bank foldings. I remember seeing him a few times when I wasn't more than a kid. He looked like he pissed ice water. Nobody knows where his money went; it just disappeared."

"Wasn't there an investigation?"

"Sure. They found out the bank went bust because Timmerman creamed it, but they never found his stash. Some claim he anticipated the Crash and was trying a hedge, but they never figured out what it was."

I thought I caught a gleam of greed in Howie's eye.

"That's very interesting." He drank some coffee, wiped his mouth with his fingertips and gazed beyond me. "Maybe there's some connection. Wasn't Mrs. Bonney pretty well off?"

"I don't think she could've bought out Ford, but she wasn't missing any meals I know of."

"What'd she own besides the lake cabin?"

"A new Buick and a house in town. I don't know what else."

"What'd her husband do?"

"Peddled insurance. Died in the lake. Might have been a suicide, could've been an accident. The story I got was he tried to swim across Kampie when he was loaded and picked a rough night. Didn't make it."

"So, being an insurance man, he left his wife well off, eh?"

"Could be."

Howie took off his glasses with both hands, polished them with a linen handkerchief and gazed at me nearsightedly before putting them on again.

"What about the mother?"

"I hear she was a knock-out. Died young. Before Timmerman shot himself."

"Apparently no one dies of old age in that family."

"I've known luckier tribes."

The sour waitress came by and grudgingly poured more coffee. Howie didn't notice her and burned his tongue when he absent-mindedly took another sip.

"Damn, I wish they wouldn't sneak around you like that," he muttered, taking a cold drink of water. After a few seconds of gloom he asked what Kate looked like.

"Big eyes, real blue, little nose, slim waist, a tight ass. She moved quick and was bossy, like my ma, only she talked like a man. Husky voice, and cussed a lot."

"You ever make a pass at her?"

"Never had a real chance. Might've if I'd been her bootlegger or iceman."

"Maybe she was too slim for you."

"Live ones don't get too slim for me. Or too round either. Now fat I'm not crazy about, and I mean real, sloppy, greasy fat—"

He waved his hand while giving me a pained look and I quit, satisfied with making him sorry he'd asked.

"What'd Kate do after she was widowed?"

"All I know is she bought moon from Boswell, lived in the cabin summers and in town winters. She either drank a lot or had a mob of friends who did because she kept Bos busy."

"What we need is to find someone who really knew her."

"Fine, let's get started."

"You get started," said Howie. "I've got paying clients to think about. You're Boswell's great and true friend and you're the murder-solver so this is just your cup of tea. Go find out who did it and maybe I can get your friend off."

"Come on, you don't really think they'll try to nail Boswell for killing her, do you?"

"Absolutely. But don't worry. I have faith in you."

He had faith in me. That made one of us.

I walked through the bright heat back to the police station, hoping I'd find a cop I knew, but there was only the desk sergeant who looked as old and unfriendly as my pa when I walked up and asked who was in charge of the Bonney murder case.

"Who're you?" he asked in a bullfrog voice.

I told him. He wrote it down.

"Address?"

I told him that. He looked up at me. "Wilcox. From Corden. Your old man runs the hotel there, right?"

"Uh-huh."

He grinned, showing me pale-gummed dentures.

"You lasted three rounds with a carny slugger a few years back. Floored him twice—"

"He tripped over the referee one of those times."

"Some referee. You should've decked *him*."

"I tried, but he was faster than the fighter."

"That was some brawl. I never saw faster hands than you showed that night. You'd ought to've been a pro."

"Too lazy. Who'd you say was handling the Bonney thing?"

The light of excitement left his pale blue eyes and he frowned.

"That's Lieutenant Baker."

"Could I talk to him?"

"I wouldn't advise it. He never saw you fight."

"I just want a couple minutes. I know old Boswell, the guy he's holding."

The sergeant sighed, got up and told me to wait at the desk, then creaked his way back to the lieutenant's door.

A moment later he was back.

"He'll give you about a minute. Don't push it. He's feeling meaner than owl shit."

"Thanks."

Lieutenant Baker sat behind a small desk before a large window. Hard summer light reflected off a brick wall in the alley, silhouetting his wide shoulders and sleek black hair. He didn't speak as I moved the chair which faced the windows and placed it against the wall to his left.

"Carl Wilcox," he said in a soft voice as I sat down. "You stuck up a jeweler a few years back. Got convicted, went to prison. Right?"

"The gun wasn't loaded."

"Yeah, but were you sober enough to know it at the time?"

"I emptied it while I was sober, before I went on the job."

He leaned forward, resting his elbows on the desk and turned his head slightly to face me. Thick-lensed glasses magnified his cold gray eyes, which went over my carcass slowly, as though he were estimating my age, weight and shoe size.

"So what've you been doing since you got out?"

"I've been staying out. You mind if we talk about the Bonney case?"

"Why? You got the answer?"

"I know Boswell, the guy you're holding. So does Joey Paxton, Corden's cop. I just wanted to ask you to give Joey a call. He can tell you about Boswell."

"I suppose he buys his booze from that bum too?"

"Bos isn't a bum. He's a retired railroad man who makes a little money with a good still, and he doesn't kill people."

"What're you—his partner?"

"I'm his friend."

He stared at me. The eyeglass magnification blurred out all details, but his bushy brows began crowding together, forming a deep V over his nose so I knew he was glaring. "Okay, friend." He pulled his elbows off the desk and straightened up. "If you want to help your buddy, just butt out. I'll handle this case, and I don't need any goddamned help from ex-cons."

I stared at him, trying to figure out why he was so mad. His face had turned red and his voice was tighter than Queen Victoria's corset. Finally I sighed, got up went to the door and stopped.

"Do yourself a favor, Lieutenant. Call Joey Paxton."

He said nothing, just sat there behind his gogglelike glasses. I closed the door and left.

Chapter II

Kate's cabin squatted under cottonwoods and elms on the south side of Lake Kampie just three lots east of where County Road Nine connected with the road circling the lake. It was painted green in contrast with its white neighbors and had a low, tarpaper roof. Kate's fine black Buick stood in the back lawn. I parked beside it, got out and walked over the dry, sparse grass which scrunched underfoot as I approached the back door. A movement to my right halted me.

"You looking for Kate?"

I turned to face a red-haired girl with pale skin and freckles, standing at the southeast cabin corner, studying me with bright green eyes. Overalls and a gray sweatshirt hung loosely on her slim body. Her brown feet were bare. She looked fourteen.

"Hi. Who're you?" I asked.

"Polly Erickson."

"Any relation to Leif?"

"I've been asked that before," she said. "Who are you?"

I told her.

"Kate's dead. She was murdered."

"Yeah, so I heard. You live next door?"

"The police think a little old tramp did it."

"What do you think?"

"I don't know. Lieutenant Baker tried to make the old man, Kate's bootlegger, admit he did it, but he wouldn't."

"Baker was here? Did he hit the old guy?"

"No, just shook him. Real hard."

"Were you here?"

"Oh, yes. I found the body." She didn't sound proud, but the event had made her very important and she felt the responsibility. It made her solemn.

"Tell me about it."

"Were you a friend of Kate's?"

I thought of lying to make things more simple, but looking at her open, innocent face made it seem crummy, so I told her the truth.

"I'm a friend of the little old man who was here. He wouldn't kill anybody or anything. I want to help him."

"He certainly didn't look like a murderer," she said politely, "but Lieutenant Baker seemed awfully sure."

"My friend's name is Boswell. He's a retired railroad man."

"Oh," she said in a tone that conceded that was much more respectable than merely being Kate's bootlegger.

"Please tell me what happened," I said, "from the beginning."

"All right, but let's go sit on the beach in front where we'll be more comfortable."

"Lead on."

Two years of drouth had made the lakefront recede like an old man's hairline, and by that summer you had to walk half a mile to wade in a foot of water. Polly sat down and gazed at the sloping beach with its strips of pebbles alternating with smooth sand, which finally reached the water about three rods away. Across the lake, distance flattened the low hills into prairie from our view. All the sky was faded blue.

"I noticed the bootlegger—Mr. Boswell?—came before dark," she began. "I'd seen him before quite a few times. Just after he came I went to the store for my father, and I was gone quite awhile because I stopped and had a Coke with friends. Daddy doesn't care if I take a while as long as I don't go joy-riding, you know? Anyway, when I got back, I noticed the bootlegger's truck was still in the backyard and so was Kate's Buick, but there was no light in the cabin. That seemed awfully strange because on a Saturday night there's either company—lots of it—or Kate goes out somewhere, and she always drove. It just didn't seem likely anybody'd come and pick her up along with the—I mean, with Mr. Boswell."

She watched me as she talked and immediately caught my reaction to her calling Bos a bootlegger.

"What I thought, was, lots of people have been poisoned by moonshine and maybe that'd happened to them. So I came over and looked in the windows. I wasn't worrying about anything going on with Kate and such an old man, and it was light enough so I could see inside and there were Kate's feet, sort of spraddled, you know? Everything beyond was dark. So I went back to our cabin—my folks had gone to a movie in town—and I called the police. At first the man I talked to tried to put me off so I asked for Lieutenant Baker and he asked me how come I knew the lieutenant and I said because he was a friend of Kate's and probably would want to know if something was wrong with her. Right away the man said, 'You mean it's Kate Bonney,' and I said, 'Yes,' and he said someone'd be right out."

"Baker knew Kate?"

"Sure. He was stuck on her. One time he even gave her a blackjack."

So, I thought, *that's why he was all worked up.*

"He was pretty wild when he got here," said Polly. "He scared me. I thought he'd shake that old man's head off."

"Where were you?"

"Out in front, by the windows. With the light on I could see everything. Lieutenant Baker had told me to go home, but I didn't."

I grinned at her, took out my fixings and built a cigaret. Her green eyes watched every move as if I were a magician. When I lit up she looked directly into my eyes.

"Would you make one for me?"

"Aren't you kind of young to be smoking?"

"I'm sixteen. How old were you when you started?"

"Less than that," I admitted and took out my bag and paper to go through the routine again, only this time I did it one-handed.

"Golly," she sighed, "could you teach me to do that?"

"Not without more tobacco than I've got. It has a way of flipping until you get the knack, and it's tough picking shreds out of sand."

She examined the cigaret, stuck it in her mouth and accepted a light. After the first drag she blew smoke out quickly and smiled. Her teeth were quite straight and pure white.

"Actually I'm only fifteen," she confessed.

"You could pass for more if you had on shoes," I assured her.

"Being thirteen is the worst. Everybody hates you when you're thirteen, at least if you're a girl."

"Same for boys. How well did you know Kate?"

"Pretty well. She invited me in a lot, especially when I offered to dust and cut vegetables and stuff like that when she was getting ready for a party."

"She ever give you a smoke?"

"No. She said it was a stupid, filthy habit, even though she did it all the time. It'd hang from her lip and she'd squint against the smoke."

Polly did an imitation and when smoke got in her eyes, jerked the cigaret from her mouth and blinked.

"Did she talk to you?"

"Sometimes. It wasn't so much she talked *to* me, she just talked. I wanted her to tell me about things that'd happened in her family—there was lots of tragedy, you know—but she went on about things like Hoover and Roosevelt and hard times. It got a little boring except most of the time she said real funny things. I wanted to hear about how her father had killed himself and how she lost the two fingers."

"She was shy two fingers?"

"Uh-huh. On the left hand. Not the whole fingers, just part of the little pinky and the one next to it."

"You ever find out how it happened?"

"*She* never told me. I heard somewhere that it was an accident when she was little." Polly glanced back toward the cabin, hitched her bottom a couple times so she was closer to me and narrowed her green eyes. "*I* don't believe it was any accident."

"Why not?"

She straightened up, pulled her head back and frowned at her shrunken cigaret.

"Lots of reasons. They said some kid did it by accident when she was at camp, but no one knew who the kid was. But from things Kate said, I'll bet her father would've told everybody in the world who it was and made a real big fuss. The story is that nobody wanted to upset the kid's parents or ruin the kid's life."

"How'd you hear all this? Wasn't that a long time ago?"

"Mom told me about it. She didn't like Kate much, didn't want me hanging around over there. She thought something was real bad with all of Kate's family—too many people killed and stuff like that. Actually I think it was mostly that Mom thinks women who smoke are awful and drinking's worse."

"So what do you think happened to the fingers?"

"You won't tell?"

"Never."

"I think it was her dad."

I lifted my eyebrows. "Why'd he do that?"

"Well, I'm not saying he did it on purpose. But she hated him. I *know* that. You could tell by the way she talked about him. She was glad he killed himself. She never came out and said it like that, but I could tell. I think maybe he killed himself because he hurt her and felt guilty, not because he lost all the bank's money."

I nodded thoughtfully and let her think it sounded reasonable because obviously she'd given it all a lot of thought and had never considered confiding her ideas with an adult before. She took another drag on the cigaret, holding it delicately with her fingertips close to the end so they came in contact with her lips when she puffed.

"It tastes nice," she told me. "I wish a person could just smoke the whole thing away so there'd be no butt left to smell up ash trays."

"You could smoke a pipe."

"They get too hot."

I shook my head. "I guess you've tried about everything."

"I've never smoked a cigar."

"Good. Tell me more about Kate."

"Well, she liked hard work and she hated for anybody not to do things her way—you know, all in a rush. She cut all the wood for her fireplace, split it and stacked it. She was real strong."

"Ah, so it doesn't make much sense, does it, that a little old man could strangle her?"

She shoved her cigaret butt into the sand and buried it.

"I don't know. Lieutenant Baker said she was strangled from behind by somebody who put a piece of twine around her neck. He said that wouldn't take anybody very big or strong."

"It'd take somebody quick and determined. Young, healthy people don't die that easy."

"Well, she might've been asleep."

"Was she the kind that dozes off after a couple drinks?"

"Oh, no. She never napped and she was up all hours. It's hard to imagine her ever going to sleep, even on purpose."

"That's what I figured. And Boswell's the last guy in the world who'd sneak around and strangle a woman from behind. He spent his whole life on the railroad, minding his own business and not so much as having a fight with a brakeman, and then he retired and took a job janitoring at the high school until this nit principal heard he let kids sneak smokes in the boiler room and got him fired. He hasn't got an enemy or a want in the world. Why'd he all of a sudden turn killer and thief?"

Polly gave that some serious thought and finally shook her red curls.

"I guess I don't know. I'll tell you, though, sometimes Kate could be pretty snotty. When she got mad she didn't care what she said and she could get mad about the littlest things."

"That wouldn't bother Bos. Anytime anybody gets nasty about him, he just blinks and lets it pass. Never even got mad at the damned principal who got him fired. Everybody in town said the guy stank except Bos."

Out on the water a white speedboat suddenly appeared from the north and cut west in front of us, skimming over the rippling blue. Polly watched a moment, then tucked her slim legs in tight and smoothed a place in the sand with her open palm. Her fingers were slender and tapered.

"Was Baker the first cop to show last night?" I asked.

"Uh-huh. I was waiting by the back door when he drove up with another policeman and he told me to go home. He didn't thank me for calling or anything. When I'd seen him at Kate's parties he was real friendly and laughed and talked to me when he came early and I was working in the kitchen. He called me Red. Kate told him once to quit flirting with me."

"Was she mad?"

"No, she was only teasing," Polly said.

"You think she liked him pretty well?"

"She liked him some, I guess, but not a lot. I mean,

she made fun of him lots of times behind his back and sometimes even to his face."

"How'd he take that?"

"I don't think he liked it at all, but he only laughed."

That was interesting. "Did she like other guys?"

"Sure, about the same way. She didn't take any of them very seriously."

"Did Baker rough up Boswell any, besides shaking him?"

"The shaking was enough, and he looked at him like he hated him—"

"More than likely he did. Cops are very moral people sometimes."

She gave me a narrow-eyed look. "I guess you don't like policemen much, huh?"

"I can take them when they leave me alone. So Kate didn't have any regular fellow?"

"I don't think so. Just a lot of interested ones. I said once it looked like she could just take her pick and she laughed and said they were only after her money."

"Did she have that much?"

"She was just being sarcastic, or maybe ironic. She was both a lot. Especially about men. She was hardly ever nice to them for long."

"You said your mother didn't like her. How about your dad?"

She turned her head and looked at me sideways. "He hardly ever saw her. He's a traveling salesman and only gets home on weekends and Kate was always busy weekends. You'll never be able to make a suspect out of my dad."

"Okay, Polly, but I have to check out all the possibilities don't I?"

She faced me straight once more and grinned. "That's all right, I understand. I guess maybe you want I should tell you *my* alibi—only I don't have one. Like I told you, I was home alone. I suppose I was the last one to see her alive except for the old man and the person who killed her."

"But your parents were home until you came back with the car, right?"

She nodded. "But you can't see Kate's cabin from ours unless you go outside. There aren't any windows on that side—that's where we have our fireplace."

We heard the car pulling in behind the cabin at the same time and rose together, like a young couple caught on the couch by returning parents.

"Maybe the police are coming back again," said Polly.

We walked around to the parking area and found a green Chevvy beside my truck. The cabin's inside back door was open, and as I started to approach, the screen door was shoved aside by a sandy-haired, stocky man who walked duck style and carried his arms wide like a fat man or a weight-lifter. Before he looked up and saw us his face drooped sorrowfully; he looked at least fifty. Then his head came up, his small blue eyes took us in and a beaming smile made him young. It was the smile of a successful politician, perfectly sincere, telling you he was glad to see you, anxious to know you, eager to help. All Santa Claus.

"I'm Sig French," he announced, "Kate's only cousin. You must be neighbors, eh?"

"I am," said Polly, and gave her name.

"Polly!" beamed French. "I've heard about you. You're just as pretty as Kate said in her letters!"

Polly blushed and dipped her curly head as Sig moved

closer and reached for my hand. His grip was firm, warm and padded. His expression became mournful.

"This is a terrible thing. What happened? You a friend of Kate's?"

"Can't say I was. Name's Carl Wilcox. I'm a friend of the old man the police found in the cabin when they came out."

He didn't flinch or drop my hand, just released it naturally and peered at me, taking in the broken nose, floppy black hair and dark jaw.

"Yeah. Lieutenant Baker mentioned you. Said you might come around. I'll have to say that after seeing your old friend, I can't help but think it's impossible he had anything to do with it. I mean, how the devil could he kill a woman as strong and active as Kate? Even if he had reason?"

"Well, now, I'm glad to hear you say that."

"I said it to the lieutenant. I don't think he liked it, but I said it anyway. Of course I wasn't about to tell him his business—"

"How'd you happen to see Boswell?" I asked.

"When the lieutenant told me about things, I asked if I could and he took me back to the cell. Good heavens, that man must be at least seventy-five and not much taller than five-four, right?"

I nodded.

"And he'd delivered moonshine to Kate every week for years, isn't that right?"

"Right again."

"Well! It had to be someone else!"

"That's the way I see it. Could we talk some? I'd like to learn more about Kate and—"

"You bet, but not just now, Carl. My wife, Lorna—she's inside—she's pretty shaken up about all

this. Needs a little time to get, you know, adjusted. And
the truth is, we been pretty much out of touch. I don't
know hardly anything about Kate's life in the past few
years. I'll be glad to give you family background and
stuff like that if it'll be any help. And, Carl, I want to
help. It's silly, I know, but when a relative dies and
you've been out of touch, you feel guilty, right?".

I don't, but he was so eager and open it seemed
mean to contradict him and I just nodded. He went on
a little, became aware that he was getting tiresome,
broke off, apologized, told us he was glad we'd met and
suggested I come back in a day. Something in his man-
ner suggested that he had serious troubles in the cabin.
I guessed he was afraid of his wife.

After he shook hands with us again and went inside,
Polly walked with me to my truck.

"Seems like a nice fella," I said.

"Uh-huh."

I looked at her. "You don't sound impressed."

"I don't believe Kate ever wrote to him about me."

"Why?"

"She never wrote letters. She told me so."

"So he told a white lie to make you feel good. Is that
so bad?"

"He said it to make me think he was nice. Just like he
told you he thought your friend didn't kill Kate. I bet
he made the lieutenant think he was right in suspecting
Boswell."

I thought that over for about a second and nodded.
"Maybe you'd ought to solve this murder. You see
more than I do."

She gave me a look that suggested flattery wasn't going to get me anywhere either. I opened the truck door,
climbed inside and looked down at her.

"You know anybody else I could talk to about Kate? Any close friends that came to parties?"

She frowned a moment, then nodded.

"Try the Ryders. They live east, right before the waterworks. It's a cabin built into a little knoll, kind of apart. Her name's Avril. She was Kate's best friend. She makes beer and angel food cake and can chin herself twenty times."

That sounded like an unbeatable variety of talents and I asked what such a fantastic woman had for a mate.

"Oh, he's just fat and funny."

"You like him?"

"I don't not like him."

That put him one up on Sig French, I decided, but fell pretty shy of being an endorsement.

I drove in shade for about a quarter of a mile before the trees thinned out and there was nothing but burned prairie on the south and whitecapped lake on the right. As Polly had said, the Ryder cabin was set well apart and from the road looked small, tucked into the knoll that overlooked a bay where the shoreline curved north. A one-car garage had been tunneled into the embankment to the east of the cabin's rear entrance and I parked in front of the closed door.

Even before I got out of the truck I guessed no one was home. It seemed that maybe no one had ever lived there, except the stink of ripening garbage was strong from cans beside the stoop as I stepped up and rapped on the door. The only answer was the moaning wind.

Fresh out of leads and patience, I got in the truck and drove back to the hotel in Corden for free lunch.

Chapter III

Bertha probably isn't a third cousin to a hump-backed whale as I've claimed. Her temperament's no where near as gentle and she doesn't have flukes, but she's big enough to raise the water level in Lake Kampie to its old banks if she'd go wading, and watching her move between the ranges and the serving table in the Wilcox Hotel is enough to make a man believe in miracles. The temperature under the pressed iron ceiling averages near a hundred on a normal South Dakota summer afternoon, but Bertha doesn't sweat. Her round face turns red as a thermometer butt, she keeps shoving her stringy black hair back, and she never takes a step she doesn't have to. My nephew claims that back before Ma closed the dining room, he'd watched Bertha serve meals through an evening rush when she never moved her right foot from where she kept it for a pivot.

When I walked into the kitchen, she was sitting at the little table beside the windows that overlook the clotheslines in the gravelly backyard.

"Do you always come late for meals to provoke me or just to avoid eating with your ma and pa?"

"It's so I can have you to myself."

"Horseapples," she scowled.

"I'll fix my own sandwich, okay?"

She said I was damned right I would and let me
know what she'd do about my manhood if I left so
much as a crumb to soil her counter when I was
through. Ordinarily I'd have hung around kidding with
her for a while, but I was anxious to get some notion
about how townspeople were reacting to Boswell's
troubles, so I ate and meandered down to Bond's Café
for the local gossip. Several folks came around to ask
what was happening. Nobody believed he'd killed Kate,
or at least none would admit it to me.

Joey Paxton, our hound-faced cop, dropped by, and
I asked him if Lieutenant Baker had called to ask about
Boswell.

"What makes you think he'd ask me?"

"Wouldn't it be a natural thing to do? Check out the
man's record?"

"It might be the *normal* thing to do. Baker hardly
ever does the normal thing. You didn't suggest he call
me, did you?"

I admitted I had.

"So he didn't. Not right away. He probably will later.
He's independent as a hog on ice."

"How about if you called him?"

He gave me his sorrowful stare, shook his head and
cradled his coffee cup in both hands as if they needed
warming.

"What you'll need to do," he said, "is find another
suspect. Somebody you can point to without him knowing it was you that pointed. Baker's great on convictions
and credit. He don't care a whole lot about anything
else as far as I know."

"I hear he cared about Kate, even romanced her
some."

"A man can romance a lady without he cares a whole

lot about her, just as long as it doesn't keep him from
doing what he thinks is important."

"How smart is he?"

"Oh, he's smart enough, he just don't like to compli-
cate things. He'd rather travel a straight line, everything
simple. Maybe that don't make him one of your bright
fellas, but it don't make him dumb."

I walked back to the hotel and found my old man
standing beside his yellow canary's green cage, grinning
as the bird sang. As far back as I can remember, Elihu's owned canaries and they've always sung their fool
heads off. This one, named Eldridge, was no exception.

"Ain't he a corker?" Elihu asked me.

"Eh?" I yelled, cupping my ear. "That bird's making so much racket I can't hear you."

"How about you haul out the trash and burn it," he
yelled back. "Can you hear that?"

Since I was hoping to borrow his Dodge later I said
sure, did it, replaced the lower half of a shed door screen
and then touched up the front sign. As we walked
toward the kitchen for supper I popped my question.
He told me with poorly hidden pleasure that he had to
give Ma a ride to church and back, so he couldn't possibly spare it.

"That's two blocks away."

"Your ma don't walk to church."

"Oh, I forgot. God can't stand people that sweat."

It was near seven o'clock when I wheeled my asth-
matic truck into the Ryder's back lot. The garage door
was still closed, but encouraged by the sight of a curtain
stirring on the second floor, I walked to the screen door
and knocked.

After my second knock the inside door opened. A

man loomed before me like a reared-up grizzly—a bald one, if you can picture that.

"Mr. Ryder?" I asked.

"Cop?" he asked back.

"No."

"Positive?"

"Do I look like a cop?"

"No, you're too small. But you can't be a salesman, you're not wearing a tie."

"Yeah, and I'm too late to be the milkman. Look, if your name's Ryder I'd like to talk to you for a few minutes, okay?"

"About what?"

"Kate Bonney."

He stared at me a second, then said, "Why?"

"I understand you're a friend of hers."

"Yeah? Where'd you get that notion?"

"One of her neighbors told me."

"That Erickson woman, I suppose. Or was it Polly—the kid with red hair and green eyes."

I admitted it was Polly.

"What the hell does a green-eyed kid know?" he demanded.

"She probably knows she hasn't got blue eyes. You mind if we quit kidding around and talk about Kate?"

"Yeah, I mind. I don't want to talk about her."

"What've you got against Kate?"

"I haven't got anything against her. She wouldn't let me put anything against her and I wouldn't if she did. You must be a cop. What's going on?"

"My name's Wilcox. I'm a friend of a guy who's been nailed for killing Kate, only he didn't do it—"

Ryder leaned forward and raised a massive paw.

"Somebody killed Kate? Is that what you said?"

He leaned closer, brushing the screen with his forehead, which towered over me. I got a whiff of alcohol
and stared up at tufts of hair that sprouted around his
ears like little wings. Tight wrinkles crowded his bulging
eyes and his nose jutted toward me, pink and smooth,
bristling with nostril hairs. His mouth was froggish, his
teeth even and yellow.

When I told him yes, he pushed the screen open,
took my arm and pulled me inside.

"Jesus H. Christ, you're not shitting me? Jesus
Christ. Come inside. Tell me what happened."

He led me through a cramped vestibule into a wide
room lined with bookshelves and cabinets anywhere
there wasn't a window. Hulking wood and leather
chairs, couches and tables cluttered the place, making it
look like a furniture salesroom.

"You want a drink?" he demanded. "By God, I do.
Sit down someplace. Who'd you say you were?"

I told him again and he nodded, apparently without
listening, and lumbered over to a cabinet which he
opened, revealing a bar. Under the top shelf I saw gallon cans perfectly fitted into a space designed for them.
Then he was filling glasses from a fancy glass decanter
kept on the top shelf.

"You want water?"

I said a little.

What he put in wouldn't float a piss ant, but the
moonshine was quality so I didn't mind.

We sat in leather cushioned chairs flanking the fireplace, which had kindling neatly piled beside it nearly a
yard high. He leaned toward me, listening and blinking
as he drained his glass with absent-minded gulps. Al-
though his lap was filled with belly, he didn't strike me
as a sloppy fat man. His neck was thick with muscle, his

shoulders sloped, but looked a yard wide, and the big tumbler shrank to a shot glass between his huge hands.

"Jesus," he said, shaking his head when I ran down. "This is gonna kill Avril. She thought the world of Kate. They were like sisters—"

"Is Avril your wife?"

He looked startled, then grinned slyly and shook his head again. "My little sister. She's out on the lake, rowing someplace. Takes our boat and sits on the lake at night. Likes the moon or something."

"Just the two of you live here?"

"Just through the summer. Where's your home?"

"Corden."

"Ah! And the name's Wilcox. You related to the hotel people there?"

"Elihu's my old man."

"No shit? That white-haired old patriarch—beak nose, stubborn jaw, ramrod back? Looks like a goddamned Prussian. You sure don't take after him, do you?"

"Not so's anybody's noticed."

He gave me his frog grin and leaned back.

"Don't get along with him worth a damn, do you?"

"Not too bad—"

"Don't try to con me. Fathers never like sons that don't take after them. Never really believe they did the fathering—"

"You mind if we talk about Kate?"

"Yeah, I do. We're in my place, so I get to ask the questions unless you're a cop, and you admitted you're not."

"I'm trying to get some help—"

"Okays, guys that want help talk polite, chat about the family—"

"So how's your family?"

"Haven't got one. Don't even know who bore me, only who bores me."

"Then how come you know Avril's your sister?"

He grinned so broadly I could see a gold crown on a lower left molar.

"You sound like a cop. Caught that right away, didn't you? Okay, we'll talk about Kate. She was shaped like a woman, thought 'like a man, worked like a fool and swore like a muleskinner. She didn't like men because she hated her pa, and she especially hated ugly fat men, so she couldn't stand me and I wasn't exactly nuts about her. I'd never have had the nerve to try killing her because if I missed I'd know damned well she'd cut my nuts off. She was a bloody terror, that's a fact. But she liked Avril, so I put up with her when I had to."

"How often was that?"

He stared into his empty glass and sighed. "Too bloody often. Sometimes I wasn't sure whether she stuck around because she really liked Avril or because she loved badgering me. She was a badgering woman, you know. Never ignored anybody she didn't like. Made a habit—hell, a practice—of worrying you. Like a cat—you know how they'll hang around to give you the creeps when they know you hate them?"

He struggled up and offered to take my glass, but I pulled it back, saying I was fine. He built a new drink and wandered over to look out the windows into the deepening night.

"Avril's down at the dock," he said. "Why'd anybody want to sit on a dock that's half a block from the goddamned water?"

"You said Kate and Avril were like sisters. They

know each other a long time?"

"Hell, yes. Went to school together. Always pals—when they weren't fighting. Kate fought everybody. Goddamned wildcat. 'Course Avril's no saint herself. They'd have spitters every so often, but mostly it was pals."

"What got them spitting?"

"Christ knows. What difference does it make?"

"I'm trying to find out why Kate got killed. You make it sound like just about anybody close might've done it, or wanted to."

"Well, not Avril. She never so much as belted Kate, and God knows she asked for it more than once."

He took a good swig from his glass, turned and smiled at me. It looked open and friendly as a tail wag, but I didn't think the man behind the smile was all that happy about me.

"Why don't you go down and talk with Avril?" he suggested. "If you want to know about Kate, she can tell you."

"I'm not all that keen about telling her her friend's been murdered."

"Better you than me," he said cheerfully. "And what could put you in a better way to hear what a sweetie Kate was?"

I finished my drink, put the glass on the table beside me and got up.

"Okay, show me the way."

He took me down a flight of stairs off the kitchen and through a furnished basement room that let out on a sloping lawn overlooking the beach.

I didn't hear the door close behind me until I'd walked a rod or so across the brittle grass. I felt that Ryder was afraid for me to talk with the woman out there, but if so, why'd he tell me where she was and suggest I join her?

The figure slumped on a highbacked bench at the dock's end was sharply silhouetted against the glassy lake surface, which still held light from the fading sky. I stepped up from the beach and walked slowly, feeling a gentle sway of the planking underfoot. About a yard from the woman I stopped.

"Hi," I said.

Her shoulders twitched and then her cropped head turned slowly to face me. Her face was a pale glow with two deep shadows in the upper half.

"Your brother said you wouldn't mind if I came down to talk with you. My name's Wilcox. Carl Wilcox."

"I don't have a brother," she said. Her voice was husky.

"I've got some bad news." She turned her face back toward the lake. "Kate Bonney was murdered last night."

For a moment she didn't speak or move then her head lowered. "I know."

"Yeah? How come your brother didn't?"

"I *told* you, I don't have a brother. You've been talking to that idiot, Ryder. He doesn't know *anything*."

I considered that for a moment, decided it wasn't worth pursuing and took a step closer.

"Look, would you mind telling me a little about Kate? I hear you were real close."

She turned her head towards me. "Are you a cop?"

"No. I'm an old friend of the guy who was found in Kate's place when cops got to the cabin. Maybe you know him. He sold moonshine to Kate for several years."

"Old Boswell?"

"Yeah."

"My God, Baker said they caught a tramp they were sure killed her, but Boswell! That's idiotic."

"That's what I figure. So will you help me out?"

She straightened up and examined me.

"Who'd you say you are?"

I told her again.

"I've never heard of you."

"I'm only famous in my own family."

"Well, sit down, but don't expect much. Right now I'm in a hell of a way. I don't really feel like talking."

I moved around the bench and parked about a yard to her left. She had given up trying to see what I looked like in the dark and turned her gaze out on the distant lake.

"It used to be I'd sit here with water all around, and if there was a breeze, little waves'd come in from the west and I'd feel like I was floating on a tall raft, sailing across the lake. Now you can hardly see the water, and I suppose in four or five years there won't be so much as a muddy spot out there. The whole miserable state's drying up. Everything's going to hell."

"Yeah. When'd you hear Kate was dead?"

"Baker called me this morning."

"The police lieutenant?"

She nodded, pulled her right leg up and hugged it against her breast.

"Why didn't you tell Ryder?"

"Why should I? He never liked her. He might've gloated."

"Did he hate her?"

"Don't be ridiculous." She released her leg, shoved both feet out on the dock and rested her arms along the bench back. Her left hand extended just behind my shoulder.

"Do you know anybody that hated her?" I asked.

She shook her cropped head.

"Did she keep money around the cabin, or have jewelry worth anything?"

She shook her head.

"How about guys—any she was having trouble with?"

She said no loud enough to startle herself, sat up straight, turned sidesaddle on the bench and leaned toward me.

"Look, I don't really want to talk right now. I feel all numb. I should be bawling, but instead I feel sore all over. I know I should feel sorry for old Boswell and helpful toward you, because it's wonderful for that old man to have a great and good friend and all that crap, but right now I haven't got any sorry to spare. That's the way it is. I would just like to be left the hell alone."

"I heard Kate was a lesbian. Were you one of her lovers?"

She froze for a moment, then settled back, rested her left arm on the bench back and stared at me.

"Well, you're really something, aren't you? Was that supposed to shock me out of feeling sorry for myself and make me spill my guts?"

"It seemed worth a shot. But I did hear it. I mean that she liked girls better than guys. Nobody's told me you went to bed with her."

"Well, that's nice."

"Is Ryder your brother?"

"No, for Christ's sake. I've already told you that twice."

"Why does he call you his sister?"

"He wouldn't know if he had a sister. He's a bastard. A real one. Unmarried mama. Mine was married as hell. Goddamn but she was married. I cook for Ryder, okay?"

"So you aren't married to him or anything?"

"What the hell do you mean—or anything?"

"Do you sleep with him?"

"Why the hell would I sleep with that fat bastard?"

"Who knows why anybody sleeps with anybody? I'm trying to find out if Ryder had reason to be jealous—or thought he did."

"He didn't, not either of those. You're barking up the wrong tree, so why don't you just scram? I don't want to talk anymore."

"Are you going to bawl?"

"I might. Whether I do or not is none of your god-damned business and you can just stop trying to pump me—"

"Okay, this is a lousy time. How about tomorrow?"

"I don't know."

"I'd sure appreciate it. Right now there's nobody but you I can get a lead from."

A light suddenly hit us from the cabin and I twisted around to see the back door open and Ryder looming black against the inside light.

Avril paid it no attention; maybe she didn't even notice the light.

"I think Ryder's worried about his cook," I said.

She didn't respond so I stood up. "See you tomorrow?"

"All right."

The anger and huskiness had gone from her voice. She was only miserable. I walked back on the swaying dock, crossed the beach and approached Ryder who stood, huge and dark, in the doorway.

"Well," he said, "that took long enough. You must know all there is to know about Kate by now."

For a moment, as I approached, I had the notion he was going to block my way through the cabin and back to my truck. I wished I could see his eyes. The voice had something in it that bothered me but I couldn't figure what it was. At the moment I guessed it was jealousy or plain hate.

I halted two feet in front of him.

"You want me to walk around the cabin instead of through?"

Immediately he became apologetic, stepped back, waved me in and turned to lead the way. When I climbed into the truck outside he stood nearby. Faint light from the windows above touched his heavy face.

"I suppose you'll be back," he said.

"If you don't mind."

"You'll be back, whether I mind or not."

"Why do you say that?"

"I know about you, Wilcox."

"Yeah? Like what?"

"Enough. I do mind if you come back. It'd be better if you just left us alone."

With that he turned and walked back to the cabin. I realized then what I'd heard in his voice. It was fear.

I started the truck and drove back to Corden.

Chapter IV

It was some past noon when I drove back to the lake on Sunday morning. Hot wind whipped my gravel dust tail off the road and across the burnt fields, and I was glad I only met a couple cars which rattled by, laying dust on me and taking their share as the drivers glared through their hastily rolled up windows.

I pulled into Kate's back lot, feeling dusty, hot and ornery.

At once Sig appeared behind the back-door screen and the next moment he was coming out to greet me. His Santa smile was bigger than ever and he looked disgustingly cool in white ducks and a white shirt.

"Hot on the road, eh? Like a nice glass of water? Maybe some lunch? We're just sitting down to eat—"

I managed to apologize for the bad timing, turned down the lunch and said I'd take water. He led me through the small back shed into the kitchen, which felt cool and smelled strongly of coffee and faintly of flowers.

"Lorna," called Sig as he chipped a piece of ice from the block in the icebox for my drink. "Mr. Wilcox is here."

Her answer was so low I couldn't tell whether it was

"Oh" or "So what?" but after Sig filled the water glass from the small pump beside the sink, I followed him into the living room.

Lorna French looked like a mouse in mourning, and her dark eyes watched me with that bright-eyed stare you see looking up from a snapped trap just before the death glaze takes over. One look was enough to tell you nothing good had ever happened to this woman, and never would. She couldn't allow it.

I said "Hi," and she gazed at me with an expression that implied I'd made a frivolous remark to a bereaved woman. Sig saved me from making any more boners by launching into a spiel about how I was trying to make sure that justice prevailed and society was avenged for the vile act perpetrated in the cabin Saturday night. It was enough to make me think I should preen a little. Lorna's reaction—or dead lack of it—didn't encourage any false pride. I looked around, wondering which chair Kate had died in.

Sig got me parked in a chair at the table, offered a sandwich and when I said no again, attacked his lunch.

"I don't believe there's anything I can tell you that will help," said Lorna. The statement seemed to give her satisfaction.

"I'd still like to talk a little about her, if you don't mind."

"I suppose I don't."

Sig stopped chewing and beamed at her.

"What was your relationship with Kate," I asked.

"She was my niece. Her father was my older brother. We were never close—my brother and I, I mean—or Kate either. He was much older than I, and of course she was much younger."

"When'd you see her last?"

"She was in the Cities last Thanksgiving. Didn't spend it with us, though. She had other friends."

"Did you know them?"

"No. Kate wasn't a sharing person. Besides, she probably didn't expect they'd be interested in us."

"But she came to see you?"

"Oh, yes. She rather cultivated my husband. They'd talk till all hours. I never could stand those all-night things—"

"Come on, Lorna," said Sig in his kindly tone. "It was never all night. Maybe a little past the witching hour, that's all."

I finished the ice water and set the glass down.

"Did she talk any about her friends in the city?" I asked Sig.

"Nope. Mostly she wanted to talk about old times, when she was growing up and all. Lorna's right that we weren't close to Kate after she grew up. But when she was real little I saw a lot of her—took her to the county fair one year and carnivals a couple times. She was a real spunky kid, pretty and smart . . ."

His throat got thick and he looked out the window towards the lake.

"She was also willful," said Lorna, and when Sig scowled at her she set her mouth a second and said, "Well, she was. She was willful all her life. And selfish—like her father."

"How'd she get along with him?"

She sniffed and Sig looked embarrassed.

"Maybe they were too much alike?" I suggested.

Sig, looking grateful, agreed.

"How'd she get along with her mother?"

"Oh, like normal—" began Sig.

"There was nothing normal about Ellen," said Lorna

sharply. "All that woman cared about was clothes, parties and men."

"Well," said Sig, "Kate and she got along, though."

"Yes, because Ellen never even tried to make her behave."

There's nothing like arguments between marrieds to make me feel good about bachelorhood, and while it was nice to see Lorna looking peevish instead of mournful, I wasn't that excited about any more of their disagreements about child-rearing, so I steered them back toward Kate's last visit.

"Did she say anything about who she was staying with or seeing in Minneapolis at Thanksgiving?"

"No," said Lorna. "She didn't offer and we didn't snoop."

After a little more of the same I gave up, thanked them for their time and water, and left.

When I parked in Ryder's drive, Avril was cleaning crappies on a table built on stakes driven into the ground about half a rod southwest of the cabin's back door. She glanced around as I got out of the truck, then turned back to the table. I stopped at her side and admired her work with the slim, dark knife. For all the effort she made, she might have been using a wand.

"I get the notion you've cleaned a fish a time or two before," I said.

"All it takes is a sharp blade."

"That must be a first cousin to a razor. Catch 'em nearby?"

"You'll never know."

She moved the last fish into a pail of water at her side, swished it around and put it with four others in another pail beside her right foot. There was a chunk of ice in the water.

She rinsed the knife, wiped it with newspaper, wrapped the entrails and carried them to a garbage pit. When she'd covered them with sand she came back, threw away her rinsewater and started towards the cabin carrying the fish bucket in one hand and the empty pail in the other.

"You willing to talk today?" I asked as I tagged along.

"Yes."

I opened the back door for her and followed as she went inside and led me to the kitchen.

"I'm going to cook these," she said. "You want some?"

"My mouth's been watering since I first saw them," I admitted.

The night before, when she'd been only a voice and shadows, I'd imagined her younger, rounder and at least semitragic. In daylight she was over thirty, tall, and while not quite horsey, she had a look of durability, what ma would call pioneer stock. Her tanned face wasn't tragic at all; she had laugh wrinkles around her blue eyes and red mouth.

When she'd placed the fish on the counter she met my eyes and grinned suddenly, showing good teeth.

"Looked better in the dark, didn't I?"

"Don't we all?"

That didn't exactly tickle her, but then she gave my face a once-over and nodded, still grinning, before she turned to lunch.

"Where's Ryder?" I asked.

"In town. Don't worry about him."

"Is he a guy I should be worried about?"

"He's a man," she said, and crouched down to pull a frying pan from under the counter. Before straightening up, she glanced at me. "Did he tell you not to come back?"

"He sort of gave me the notion it wouldn't break his heart if I got lost."

She stood up, placed the frying pan on the stove and sadly shook her head.

"I told him he was a fool to get snotty, but he can't help himself. Actually, he's a pretty intelligent guy—but he's also an idiot. I'm out of corn meal. We'll just cook these in butter."

"Why do you say he's an idiot?"

"He just never handles anything right. He knows damned well he can't get anywhere trying to boss me around, but he keeps trying, and he knows just as well that you're not a man who'll be scared off, but he still tried that. He's such an idiot he told me not to talk to you at all."

"Is that why we're talking? Just to show him?"

"No. I thought that way some last night, when we had the fight about all this, but in bed—my own—I thought of Kate and old Boswell, and I made up my mind you were right and I was going to help you every bit I could and I will."

"All the way?"

"Yes."

"Suppose I thought Ryder was a suspect?"

She stopped measuring coffee into a percolator and stared at me.

"Ryder? Why in the world—?"

"He hated her, didn't he?"

She scowled, stared at the percolator, trying to figure

out how much coffee she'd put in, grabbed the sieve out, dumped it back into the coffee can and remeasured deliberately. Then she set the teakettle full of water on the burner, lit the gas with a stove match and touched her short brown hair with one hand.

"Do you know where he was Saturday night?" I asked.

"He was playing poker in town."

"Where were you?"

"Here. Well, depending on what hour you're talking about. I went fishing for a while."

"Didn't you usually get together with Kate on weekends?"

"Not always. The fact is, she made me think she was going to be in the Cities this weekend. I don't know why she stayed at the cabin without telling me. Something must've come up to change her mind."

"Did she change her mind often that way?"

"Sure. Especially lately. She was always popping off somewhere."

"When'd you see her last?"

"Wednesday. Listen, do you mind if we just have the fish without anything else? I don't want potatoes or even a vegetable. Is that okay?"

"Fine. Tell me about this last meeting with Kate."

"Well, she just dropped by. She did that a lot, mostly when she didn't think Ryder'd be around. Since they haven't—hadn't—been getting along too well, she sort of avoided him. She knew it upset me when they got nasty with each other and it always wound up that way. Ryder's pretty quick with a nasty, but Kate could always top him and it got uncomfortable."

"She ever try to talk you into leaving him?"

She had the fish in the pan by then and the smell and

the crackling as they cooked ran me out of questions. We stood there, side by side, watching and sniffing.

"She never said it out straight, just kidded. I told her I stuck around for the lake and to take care of him. He needs me. Poor Ryder, he'd starve to death without his cook."

"I think it'd take a while."

She laughed. "That's exactly what Kate said. She told me he could live on stored fat till hell froze over."

"How'd you and Ryder get together?"

"Oh, it's awfully dull. I worked in his office. Receptionist and part-time typist. I recepted okay. That doesn't take much genius and when I'm in the mood I can be horribly friendly. Back then Ryder only weighed a quarter of a ton or so and he was always awfully funny."

She turned the fish, which had turned all gold, and the fresh side sizzled fiercely as she hastily began setting the little table by the window overlooking the road. Then she returned to stand beside the stove.

"I'd been going with a fellow at the time, a horribly good-looking, trim young son-of-a-bitch. God, he was gorgeous—black hair, dark eyes and this unbelievable profile. I should've known from the start I couldn't hold a guy like that. Women were always ogling him and hanging around with those sick calf expressions."

She moved the fish to plates, and we sat down at the table after she'd poured coffee, and started in. For a while she was too busy boning and wolfing fish to talk, and I followed suit. It was perfect. I ate three nice-sized crappies while she did two, and then we sat back, grinning, and drank coffee.

"Actually I like them best just in butter and with no

distractions. A couple fresh rolls would've been good, but I couldn't wait."

"What happened to the dream boy?"

"Don't you like to talk about food?"

"Sure, but mostly before I'm full of it. I never had better in my life, honest. What about the guy?"

"You could make me appreciate Ryder again. Okay, the rat dumped me. You could see that coming, couldn't you? And on the bounce I landed in Ryder's fat lap. Only, like I said, it wasn't that fat then. But fat enough to seem safe and dependable and fun. He stayed tolerant when I went through my moping stage and finally said for God's sake, if you can't be friendly to the goddamned customers, I'll take you home and keep you out of sight and maybe some fresh air and good fish'll turn you human again. I'd visited out here a couple times when he had parties for the clients and the staff, and I loved the place. Then the goddamned lake had water almost up to the grass line out there. Oh, sure, I knew it was a crazy move, that it'd ruin whatever reputation I'd ever had, but I was feeling self-destructive and good old Ryder was so damned understanding and sympathetic and, well, *needful*. I mean, he really needed me like that other son-of-a-bitch never would. This is all pretty damned corny, isn't it? I think I'd feel better if it seemed a little sordid, which it does; but mostly it's corny, or comic. For a long time I felt like part of a vaudeville team. I don't ordinarily blab like this to strangers, but like I told you, I made up my mind last night I was going to talk until you hollered help and we'd find out who killed Kate and get the bastard hung. Or is it hanged? Dead, anyway. I'm sorry I talk so rough. I do that when I'm embarrassed and I am. You're a good listener, aren't you? Do I get to hear the story of your life—like what happened to your nose?"

"You remind me of the two little girls, one five and the other six, who were talking about things and the six year old got sore because she figured the five year old was too smart for her age and said, 'Huh! You don't even know who made you,' and the five year old said, 'Originally, or recently?' "

She laughed so hard I felt good, figuring I might match old Ryder in the comedy line and even switch Avril to a slim, if not gorgeous, man.

"Are you telling me," she said, "that your nose was broken more than once?"

"Uh-huh. First time a kid hit me with a sling-shot rock. Bull's-eye. I was sitting on top of a barn at the time so you can see he was pretty good."

"How old were you?"

"Eight. I was older the second time and it was a boot, not a rock."

"My God, are you *always* at war with somebody?"

"Is that what Ryder told you?"

"Well, yes, but I think I'd have guessed on my own."

"I haven't lost as often as you'd guess from the map."

"Why do you fight so much? Is it because you drink so much?"

"No. I just happen to meet a lot of villains."

"At least you don't have a cauliflower ear."

"Not so far. How about we get back to Kate?"

"Okay."

She got up to empty fishbones from our plates into a garbage can under the sink and then refilled our coffee

cups. For some reason she was getting better looking all
the time and I couldn't believe just eating fish had
caused the transformation. Her hips didn't look too
skinny, just trim, and I wished she'd wear a dress once
so I could see her ankles.

She began cleaning up the dishes while she talked and
I sat at the table, smoking and drinking her coffee.

She said Kate had been the best friend in her life.
They shared the same liking for the lake, fishing, big
parties, newspapers, politics and gossip.

"We always liked or hated the same people. I mean
when we met someone new and talked about them later,
we never had to tiptoe around what we thought of the
guy or girl. We'd come right out and say something nasty or very nice and know the other one would feel the
same way. And we had common dreams. We'd meet
and find out that just the week before we'd both dreamt
about meeting Greta Garbo. Once we both dreamed
that Polly Erickson—her neighbor's little girl—had
drowned in the lake. And she nearly did! She went
swimming on a windy day and almost didn't get out. It
was fantastic—"

"How'd Kate lose the two fingers?"

"The two fingers? Oh, well, that was an accident
when she was little. She was terribly self-conscious
about them and we never talked about it. Like we never
really talked about Ryder. She'd make cracks to let me
know she hated me living with him, but she never really
teed off and worked on me. Ryder never believed that.
He figured she was after me all the time to move out on
him, but that wasn't Kate's style. She was smart enough
to know that'd just get my back up."

"Didn't she ever tell you what she did when she made
her trips to the Cities?"

"No. That always bothered me, but Kate had a way of separating her life into different compartments. You only got in where she allowed, you know? She made me do the same thing. I mean, I never told her anything personal about Ryder and me—what went on and didn't go on. It wasn't that she'd say I don't want to hear about that; she didn't have to tell me—I knew. But I did feel that something was building up that she was going to tell me. The last two weeks she was full of strange excitement. . . ."

"Any notion about what was behind it?"

She had finished the dishes and stood by the sink, wiping her hands on a small towel. Her eyes avoided mine and stared out the window towards the road.

"I don't know. I guess I thought she'd found a lover . . . that maybe she was going to move away."

"Did you figure it was a woman?"

She made a face and finally nodded.

"How'd you feel about that?"

"Well, I wasn't jealous, exactly. I mean, I saw Kate as a sister. I'm not a woman who wants to sleep with women. But we were such awfully good friends, I'd have hated seeing her get into anything like that."

"Had she been in love with any women you knew?"

"Not really. She had a couple crushes. One with a kid at the hospital, which got her fired—"

"She worked in a hospital?"

"Sure, didn't you know? After her husband drowned, Kate went to school, got a nurse's degree or whatever they get, and went to work at Pilgrim in Aquatown. She'd have been a head nurse by now if it hadn't been for the trouble."

"What happened?"

"Well, none of it was simple. Kate was so darned smart and kind of pushy, she made lots of people mad at her, doctors especially. You know how *they* are. All think they're gods and that everyone should bow and burn incense to them, and Kate found out in a hurry what a bunch of phonies they were and let them know. And most of the nurses loved her and started getting their backs up when they were treated like dirt, and there was talk about Kate being a disruptive influence. The fact she was good at her job wasn't important, of course, not when she rocked their goddamned boat. I don't know exactly how it came to a head, but there was this daughter of the medical high priest, Doc Franklin. The girl had a cutesy name I can't remember. Anyway, there was this gang of doctors, mostly young ones, who called themselves the Kill Kate Bonney Club, and they built up a story about Kate trying to seduce this kid who was like a nurse intern—you know, taking training. They pushed it because Doc Franklin was the only one in the hospital who appreciated how good Kate was."

"What'd Kate think of him?"

"Oh, she thought he was great. The only nonphony in the place. He treated patients like they were really people and didn't pretend he knew things he didn't. She got irritated with him now and then—like the time he told her she'd never turn a snotty doctor into a saint by making him look foolish. Later she laughed about it. Kate laughed about nearly everything except the business with the kid. She never laughed about that, because it let the doctors who hated her get the best of her. She felt that Doc Franklin wasn't honest when he told her she should resign and wouldn't admit it was really because they'd made him believe she was a threat to his daughter. He insisted it was because she'd become so disruptive that the hospital couldn't function properly, despite her ability."

"Did she accuse him straight out of firing her because of the daughter?"

"She might have, I don't know. It'd depend on how mad she got. Actually Kate was more likely to get screaming mad about little things. Under pressure she had fantastic control. And she liked Doc Franklin very sincerely. Even when he fired her, she didn't say anything snotty about him. She was hurt, but deep down, I think she understood that he felt he had to do it, and even if she believed he was kidding himself about the reason, she didn't turn against him for that. Kate was very fair most of the time."

"Is Doc Franklin still at the hospital?"

Avril had become pretty emotional again, thinking of Kate, and was having some trouble talking. After a moment she nodded and half-whispered, "As far as I know. He's not terribly old."

She dug a lavender handkerchief out of her slacks, stood up, walked over to the window and wiped her eyes. As she put the handkerchief away she suddenly leaned forward and stared out the window.

"Well," she said, "Ryder's home. That's funny. He almost never comes back this early—"

It's my experience that that's what they all say, and I began considering ways for a hasty exit but saw nothing at first glance that looked promising. I wondered if the fat man owned a gun.

Avril spotted my uneasiness and said, "You don't have to worry," but her tone wasn't convincing.

"Why should I worry?"

"Well, of course . . ." She looked back out the

window. "He's just sitting there in his car. The booby—he's afraid to come in. What in the world does he think?"

"Is he blocking my truck?"

"Uh, yeah."

"Well," I said, getting up, "I'd better not worry him any longer. Thanks for the fish and talk. I enjoyed both."

"What're you going to do?"

"See Doc Franklin."

"I mean, right now."

"I'm gonna ask Ryder to move his car."

"Don't start anything with him. Listen, I'll come along—"

"Huh-uh. Sit tight. You come along and he'll think he's got to look good. Don't even let him see you peeking out the window."

She didn't like it but did as I asked. I let myself out and walked across the fine gravel to Ryder's Packard. It was black, long and shiny. Ryder peered out at me and smiled. From close up I could see sweat beading his nose, upper lip and forehead. A large drop slowly ran down his round, red cheek.

"Wilcox," he said. "The poor man's private eye. How you making out?"

"Not making out at all. Still just asking questions."

"Never gonna make out asking questions. Heard that from a fella long ago. Never ask. Just take. That's how I understand you always operate."

"Depends on what I'm up to."

"Sure. You know, it's peculiar, I've heard you're a very funny guy. So how come you never make me laugh?"

"Maybe it's because I'm working on a murder.

That's hardly ever too damned funny."

"Maybe that's it. I already told you you weren't gonna get anything here. I'm not gonna tell you again."

"Good, I could get tired of hearing that. Now you want to move your hearse so I can get on my way?"

"What'll you do if I don't?"

"I don't think you want to find out."

He kept smiling and sweating. Then he started the engine, put the car in reverse and eased it back. I climbed into my truck and pulled out. When I looked back just before making the turn that took me out of view, I saw him still sitting in the Packard. He was staring at the cabin and wasn't smiling any more.

Chapter V

Nobody answered when I called Doc Franklin's number, so I gave up on Sunday and returned to Aquatown Monday. Trying to reach the doc during his working day was about as easy as stepping on your own shadow. It was especially a pain in the rear because I didn't have any base of operations in town and had to keep calling from pay phones. When I tried claiming this was an emergency a very serious young woman wanted to know if she should send an ambulance. I told her only if the doc came in it.

On my third call I got what sounded like an older woman, and I told her I had a special message for Doctor Franklin and she'd better make sure she got it straight.

"Tell him I want to talk with him about his daughter. I'm not a patient. In fact I'm damned *im*patient and I've got to talk to him."

She took it in, recited it back to me as if that were a standard call for the doc and hung up.

I sat at the drugstore soda fountain and sipped on a Coke while watching the telephone booth about two yards away. The soda jerk and pharmacist watched me suspiciously by the time I'd made the Coke last forty-

five minutes. Just as I was rolling my fourth smoke, the
bell jangled and I jumped for the booth.

"This is Doctor Franklin." The voice was bedside
gentle.

"Ever read *Doctor's Dilemma?*" I asked.

"What? Who is this?"

"What'd you think of the play?"

"I enjoyed it more than the prologue. And I hope
I like whatever point you're trying to reach. Would you
please get to it?"

"My name's Carl Wilcox. I'm working on the Kate
Bonney murder."

"You're with the police?"

"Not hardly. For me, this thing's personal. The police are holding a friend of mine, Kate's moonshiner,
Boswell. I can't believe they really believe he did it.
He's old, small and harmless as a rabbit, but he was on
the scene and they haven't got another goat."

"I see. What do you expect from me?"

"She worked in the hospital. I'm told she thought
you were first-rate, even after you fired her. I want to
find out as much as I can about her, anything that might
help me figure out why she was killed. Then maybe I
can find who did it."

"I see. Well, to begin with, I didn't fire her. Second, I only knew her professionally. She was a good—
no—an excellent nurse, intelligent, efficient and
dedicated."

"Why'd the staff hate her?"

"They didn't. Some of the doctors, especially the
younger ones, found her abrasive. She was not a
diplomat."

"I heard it was stronger than that, that the interns
and medics hated her guts."

"Where'd you hear that?"

"Her best friend, the one who said Kate thought you were so great."

"I suspect her friend exaggerates."

"She told me your daughter worked with Kate. What'd she think of Kate?"

The gentle voice took on a little frost.

"My daughter and I never gossiped about our colleagues or discussed their personal relationships."

"Did anybody ever tell you Kate was a lesbian?"

"That is not the sort of thing anyone on my staff would talk to me about. Now, Mr. Wilcox, I sympathize with your efforts on behalf of your friend, but I don't appreciate your methods and I've told you all I intend to—"

"If you didn't fire Kate, why'd she leave the hospital?"

"Her leaving was her own decision. Good-bye, Mr. Wilcox."

I said good-bye to a dead line. Doc was polite, but not fanatical about it.

Chapter VI

Hermanson's Funeral Parlor was half a flight up over Torkelson's Barber Shop which was half a flight down. The right-hand steps went up to Hermanson, the left down to Torkelson. It always seemed to me there'd ought to be something significant about those directions, but I never figured it out. The building was dark brown brick and the upstairs led to a solemn door just left of heavily draped windows. I walked under the little canopy over the sidewalk, glanced at the bright barber pole on my left, climbed the steps and went through the solemn door, making a bell tinkle overhead. Young Benjamin, Hermie's ass-kissing cousin, showed up out of the gloom and told me I'd find the boss out back. He led me down a dark hall past closed doors and opened the rear screen to the back porch. I looked down across the bare parking area in front of the alley and saw Hermie standing in the shade of an apple tree, in earnest conference with a small boy. They both looked up at me and Hermie waved.

"This is Rickie Peterson," Hermie told me when I joined them. The boy wore a blue undershirt and dark pants with tennis shoes. "He came over to borrow some apples."

I glanced at the tree and said it looked like a lot had been borrowed lately.

"Yeah, that's what I told Rick. I told him they're better when they turn red, but he doesn't agree. He likes them sour."

"Ever put salt on them?" I asked the boy.

"Salt?" He gave me a blue-eyed stare.

"Yeah, you bit out a little hunk, put some salt in the bite hole and it tastes great when you take the next bite."

"Uh-huh. And I suppose it turns the apple red?"

"No," I grinned. "It's not like putting salt on a robin's tail so you can catch him. It really makes the apple taste sweeter."

"If I wanted 'em sweet, I'd wait till they turned red."

He walked off with bulging pockets while Hermie and I grinned at each other.

"If you'd skipped the ripening gab and told him you'd stick him in the embalming room the next time you caught him in your tree, you'd stop the raiding in a hurry," I said.

"I'm not worried about the apples, I just don't want him falling and breaking his neck. So what brings you around so early? Planning a head start on your weekend drinking?"

"Would I come to a funeral parlor if I did?"

"Yeah, to this one."

"How many coffinsful you got?"

"About enough to last you a month."

"That much?"

He nodded.

I shook my head. "I don't see how you get away with it. You don't look any more like an undertaker than I look like a movie star."

"What's an undertaker supposed to look like?"

"A broken-hearted corpse. Skinny and sad."

Actually he had light brown hair, a snub nose with freckles and a jaw that started under his ears and tapered to a point you could stick in a pencil sharpener. He was only about twenty-five but already had laugh wrinkles around his blue eyes and his grin showed teeth white enough for a toothpaste ad.

"Well," he said, "my old man filled the bill so folks accept me despite my flaws."

"Yeah, that's why you get about one funeral a year."

"Right. I work about as steady as you do—in honest trade. How much moon do you want?"

"I'm not buying. Did you hear what happened to Kate Bonney?"

"Yeah. I even hear they're holding Boswell for it."

"Right. And you know damned well he didn't do it. So does everybody else. What I'm trying to do is find out who *did* do it and pinned it on Bos."

"Don't look at me. He wasn't any competition."

"Who supplies you?"

He looked at me slantwise and sober. "Smart guys don't ask questions like that."

"Nobody ever called me smart."

"They never called you stupid, either, at least not to your face. How about we go over to the café and have a cup?"

"Don't you ever drink the stuff you sell?"

"Do I look stupid? Come on."

We walked through the funeral parlor, where he stopped to tell his cousin he'd be out for half an hour, and then we strolled down the street. The sun blazed and heat waves wriggled over the gravel between the high sidewalks. The café felt cool under the overhead fans and we sat in back, away from the glare of the front windows.

After he'd ordered coffee for both of us and the skinny waitress had poured and left, Hermie leaned forward, spooned in a little brew and squinted at me as I rolled a smoke.

"Tell me about this murder."

I did. He shook his head.

"You got real trouble. That cop, Baker, he's one mean son-of-a-bitch. He's liable to hang Boswell personally. You know, I'd kind of like to see you in an alley with old Baker."

"Why? And what do you mean, 'kind of'?"

"I'd like to see him knocked on his ass a few times. The only trouble is, he might take you even if he put away his gun. He's big and damned tough."

"There's no profit in fighting cops. I'm not likely to try Baker."

"You might not have a choice if you push him. What's all this got to do with where I get my merchandise?"

"Like you said, Boswell wasn't much competition. But then again, you never know how sensitive bootleggers'll be. It dawned on me this morning I don't know a damned thing about this racket I've been helping support, and here I've got an old buddy in the profession, so maybe he can educate me a little. Now it figures that you don't have a still in town, and I seem to remember that every now and then you've been in short supply, so where does it come from? Doesn't anybody make it wholesale in South Dakota?"

"Not that I know of."

"So it all comes from Chicago or the Cities?"

"So I hear."

"What's the chance of my talking with your supplier?"

"About as good as getting elected pope."

"Why? You figure I'm a revenuer?"

"No, but my supplier might. He's a very suspicious guy."

"You could reassure him."

"God couldn't reassure him."

I smoked and we drank coffee. Hermie grinned at me. The grin made him look about eighteen years old.

"I've heard you're just in the bootlegging racket to earn money for medical school. Is that right?"

He nodded.

"How'd you get started?"

He sipped coffee, put the cup down and cradled it wih his clean white hands.

"You don't want to hear about that."

"The hell I don't. I might as well hear about something somebody'll talk about. You know I don't want any piece of your racket. I've seen all I want of big houses and bullpens. Come on, tell me, how'd you get on the gravy train?"

"Well," he began, a little reluctantly, "it's a crazy story. I was talking pre-med at Minnesota U, and when Pa died the money ran out and I decided to come home and revive the business here, and so my friends at school threw a party. It was a pretty big bash and they had booze brought in by this bootlegger most of the guys thought was a combination buccaneer, Robin Hood and evil spirit. There were all kinds of stories about him—how tough he was and the competition he'd killed. He scared us all shitless, but we were fascinated. Some guys persuaded him to stick around. I found he wasn't big and didn't look any more dangerous than a bank clerk. That was my first impression. The second was that he had nothing but contempt for any of us. No—contempt isn't it. It was more as if we didn't really exist for him—like butterflies around a rattlesnake.''

Hermie looked solemn for a moment, covered his cup when the waitress offered a refill and stared at her with blank eyes when she walked off.

"When the party began winding down I started around, saying final good-byes to guys who were still sober enough to care, and I was almost to the door when this bootlegger stopped me. I wasn't very drunk, didn't even drink much in those days, but I remember this confusion, thinking, 'This guy's too old to be a student.' I couldn't place him at all, but suddenly he'd crowded me over to a corner.

" 'Your old man owned a funeral parlor,' he said.

" 'I know.'

" 'You wanna be a doc?'

" 'That's why I came to Minnesota.'

" 'Okay,' he says, 'I got a little proposition for you. You work for me a couple years and you'll have enough dough to come back and buy the trick.'

"So I told him, 'You can't buy a medical degree. You have to earn it.'

"'Sure,' he says. 'Try earning one without the dough. You want to be a goddamned doc or don't you?'

"Well, I wanted back in school so bad it hurt, and I thought for about half a second and said, 'Okay, what do I have to do?' He said he'd see me in the morning and I went home.

"The next morning I barely remembered it all, and it scared me just thinking I might have agreed to work with that guy, because I'll tell you—when he stood right in front of me he didn't look like any bank clerk. I got up, dressed, packed and headed down the stairs, figuring I'd catch a streetcar and go to the depot. But when I came out the front door, there he was, sitting in a black Packard. He pushed the door open, said get in, and I did. By the time we reached the depot, everything was all set. I hadn't said a word, just nodded."

"He must've been quite a talker."

"It wasn't the talking. I was a little hung over and damned depressed. But I didn't feel suicidal and I was positive from the time I got into the car that saying the wrong thing to this guy would be just that. I *knew* it. He didn't make any threats. It didn't occur to him he'd have to. He was in charge, and that was it."

"You really believed he'd kill you?"

"Hell, yes. But it wasn't just that."

He rested both elbows on the table and frowned thoughtfully.

"About six weeks later we were traveling west of Corden a ways in his Packard, which had overload springs and was filled with moon. Hell, that rig could qualify as a two-and-a-half-ton truck. The whole rear end was piled with gallons of moon covered nice and neat with clothes a salesman might be carrying. We'd stop in a little town where there'd not be much more than a grain elevator, gas station, general store and church. Baltz drove, he won't get in a car unless he drives—"

He stopped talking when he realized he'd let the bootlegger's name slip, and stared down at his coffee mug.

"Just forget you heard that," he said.

"Heard what?"

He grinned weakly. "Where was I?"

"On a prairie road, somewhere between grain elevators."

"Right. Okay, in one little burg—I can't remember the name—we sold four gallons to a guy who ran a gas station—Standard, of course. This guy had an oil pit inside and at the bottom there was another hole where he stored moon. I put it in for him. What he did, was he bought a supply and then he'd go down there, out of sight, while his sidekick kept watch above, and he'd cut the moon with water from a hose he used for filling radiators. All that hidey business was more complicated than other customers did it, so my partner asked why he bothered and he answered, 'Sawyer.'

" 'Who's Sawyer?' I asked.

" 'Our cop,' says the gas guy. 'Hates booze. He sees your load and he'll stop you sure as hell. Don't tell him you sold me anything. He'll go through your car and dump every can right out in the ditch.'

"I looked at my driver and he shook his head. 'Don't worry.'

"Of course I did. And sure enough, we hardly got past the city limits when a Ford wheels up beside us and waves us to the roadside. 'Leave me do the talking, said my partner, which was just fine since I didn't have any gab handy for the occasion. So the cop climbs out of his car and walks slowly back to us. He's maybe lower middle age, built like a Mack truck, thick neck, thick head, beetle brows, flat nose, red cheeks and blue jaw. I guessed he could chew nails and spit tacks. He stopped by the driver's side, stepped on the running board, leaned his weight on it and let up quick. The car barely stirred.

" 'Nice springs,' says the cop.

"My partner nodded.

" 'From Minneapolis?'

" 'Detroit,' my partner says.

" 'I meant you, not the springs.'

" 'Me too.'

"He gave us a grin that showed square teeth so far apart they looked like a row of tombstones.

" 'That's funny,' the cop says, 'I thought all moonshine in South Dakota came from Minneapolis and St. Paul or Chicago.'

" 'I wouldn't know. I sell dry goods.'

"The cop looked at our back seat, then he looked at my driver.

" 'Uh-huh. You got a suit you'll sell me?'

" 'We only sell wholesale.'

" 'So maybe I'm gonna open a men's store.'

" 'Lemme know when you got a shop.'

" 'I will. Meantime I'm gonna take a look at what you got under all that crap in the back.'

"My driver looked up at him and said, very soft, 'No you won't.'

"That's all he said. For maybe ten seconds they stared at each other. I didn't see any change in the cop's expression, but slowly he straightened up, took his hands off the door and stepped back. I waited for him to haul out his cannon while I saw my partner's hand come out of the door pocket holding a Colt .44. I was scared shitless. Then the cop turned, walked slowly to his car, got in, made a U turn and went back to the little town. He never saw the Colt. And you know something, Carl? I felt sorry for that cop. I never saw a man beat like that. He shrank. I don't think he was a coward, either. He looked into this guy's eyes and his backbone went to jelly. I knew exactly how he felt."

"What happened on the next trip?" I asked.

"I drove alone and nobody stopped me."

"So where does old murder-in-the-eyes get his booze?"

Hermie grinned. "You won't believe me. He hijacks it all from the pros."

"Uh-huh, and I get my daily bread through prayer. How often do you see this guy?"

"Every delivery."

"Tell him I want to meet him. He might be willing to talk with an old con. I figure he's served some time."

"He has, but he won't meet you."

"Will you ask?"

"Why not?"

I said good enough and we split.

Chapter VII

It was mid-afternoon and hotter than hell on Halloween, so I decided it'd be more comfortable in the hoosegow than on the street and I went over to visit Boswell. Immediately inside the police station I met Lieutenant Baker. His black suit and gray tie would have looked right in place at the funeral parlor and his expression fit better than the suit. He glared down at me through his thick specs which made him look like a mad owl.

"I told you to butt out," he said in a tone Ma uses when she's about to lace into me. I looked up, wondering if his head looked small because it was so far away or if it was just that his shoulders were wider than an ox yoke.

"I can't even visit the prisoner?"

"No, and you can goddamned well quit snooping around asking stupid questions. Get your ass back to the hotel and hop bells."

"I'm a handy man, not a bellhop, and where'd you hear I was asking stupid questions? Did you rubber hose that out of somebody?"

"I know everything that goes on in my territory.

Now keep your nose out of my business and your ass out of this station. I'll handle this case."

"You mind if I worry about Boswell a little?"

"I don't give a damn if you worry yourself sick."

"Do you know why Kate quit work at the hospital?" I asked.

He took a deep breath, shook his head and looked more sorrowful than threatening. "Wilcox, you got more gall than's healthy."

"Go on," I grinned at him. "I don't even catch colds. How about we go someplace we can talk? I'm getting a kink in my neck looking up."

"Somehow that doesn't worry me any," he said, but to my surprise he then said, "Come on," and led me down the hall to his office where he parked his broad fanny in an antique swivel chair and propped his size thirteens on the corner of the desk. The chair I'd moved before was still against the wall and I pulled it out a couple inches, sat down, tilted back and propped my feet on the front rungs.

"How come you gave Kate a blackjack?" I asked.

"I figured it'd last longer than flowers."

He didn't grin when I laughed. "Did you think she needed protection?"

"Everybody needs protection."

"Oh, you give blackjacks to all your lady friends?"

"Did somebody tell you I had something going with Kate?" His tone was mild, his eyes were murder.

"Don't get jumpy, Lieutenant, nobody's fouled your name. I just heard you'd been to her parties and somewhere along the line, gave her a token. It made me wonder if something told you she was going to need it."

The eyes gentled some. "She used to drive a convertible. I think that's a dumb car for a woman. Any nut can just jump on the running board and move in."

We sat silent for a moment. He watched me steadily through his masking glasses but seemed more relaxed.

"You're not married, are you, Lieutenant?"

He stared at me and slowly smiled. "How many times you been questioned by cops, Wilcox?"

"A few. Why?"

"Don't pull any secondhand techniques on me. I don't like it."

I thought that over for a while. It was already beyond me why he'd switched from the bully-boy to the tolerant tough, but didn't believe he was whimsical enough to throw me in a cell for asking questions he didn't like. Sure, it was possible, but I decided it was unlikely.

"What kind of a guy was Kate's husband?" I ventured.

He leaned back, clasped his big hands behind his head and looked thoughtful.

"He was all right. Played four straight years on the first team at Central High. Never got bad hurt, never missed a minute. Tougher than owl shit. Not fast, but quick. About twice a game he'd bust through and nail the halfback before he'd hardly got his hands on the ball. Then he'd get up and hop around, telling the back he'd get him harder the next time—"

"You played on his team?"

"Yeah. Right guard, he was right tackle. Our first year we lost every game; last year we won 'em all."

"He go to college?"

"No. Went to work. We all did. He got a job from a cousin in insurance. Did all right, I guess."

"You didn't keep track much, huh?"

He shook his head. "He married Kate. Got into a crowd I never knew. . . ."

I sat still, letting him think and hoping he'd talk some more, but he wasn't a man to dream about the past. His magnified eyes came around to focus on me.

"You never went out for sports," he said accusingly.

"That's right," I confessed.

"Too small?"

"Too fainthearted."

"Uh-huh. I've heard a lot about what a pansy you are. How come you never tried fighting for a living?"

"That's not a living."

"From all I hear, it damned near has been for you. So you can't stand training and discipline. That's it, isn't it?"

The real trouble was that people owned fighters and I could never belong to anyone, but I didn't figure it was worth explaining to him.

"You're right," I said, "that's my whole life in a nutshell. Did Kate's husband ever tell you what kind of a wife she was?"

He frowned. "He had a name, you know. It was Dave. Everybody called him Davey, even after school."

"Okay, did Davey ever talk about his wife?"

"Guys only talk about their wives when they've got something they want to bitch about."

"Did he?"

He took his feet off the desk and I thought he was going to get up, but instead he turned his chair, stared out the window at the brick wall across the alley and after a moment, turned back to me.

"Wilcox, I got more to do than sit around shooting

the shit with an ex-con, now—"

"Kate really liked girls better than men, didn't she?"

For a second he stared at me, then he took a deep breath, leaned back and half-closed his eyes.

"You pick that up from Avril?" he asked pleasantly.

"It's a general notion I've picked up all along the line."

"I see. So what'd you figure I was doing, going around being friendly and giving away blackjacks?"

"A lot of guys figure lesbians are a challenge."

He put his elbows on the desk and hunched his shoulders.

"I'll tell you what, Wilcox, I wouldn't go around saying Kate was a lesbian. It won't make you popular. It could get your face smashed. She was a good wife and a decent woman. She was killed by a drunken bum buddy of yours, so don't go bad-mouthing her to save that tramp's ass. Now get the hell out of here."

"How'd she lose the two fingers on her left hand?"

"If you've been questioning every damned fool at the lake you know by now."

"Polly Erickson thinks Kate's old man did it. She says that's why Kate hated him."

"That's a lot of shit."

"Yeah," I admitted. "Anyway I shovel it, it still stinks."

"Old Timmerman was a wooden Indian, wouldn't say shit if he had a mouthful and tight enough to cut the kids arm off if it'd make him a dollar, but how could it? Besides, he never handled a tool bigger than a penknife in his life. Wouldn't know which end of an axe you cut with. Now leave off this crap and haul your ass out. I got work to do."

"Can I see Boswell?"

For a second I thought I'd over-stretched, but then he gentled like a soothed horse and calmly said why the hell not, and I said thanks and moved out.

Chapter VIII

Boswell was asleep when the sergeant let me into his cell but came alive and cheerful the moment I put my hand on his shoulder.

"Wouldn't have a flask on you?" he asked wistfully when he was up and had his glasses on.

He sighed when I shook my head.

"How're you doing?"

He made a face. "They ain't workin' me too hard." He looked around the small cell with his vacant smile and began rummaging in his pockets for his pipe and tobacco.

"How long'd you know Kate?"

"Seven, mebbe eight years. Old Ted Webster told her about me and she said for him to send me by. Been doin' it ever since."

"The first time you went over, was it to the cabin? What happened?"

"Well, I drove to the lake there and found where her place was, and then I went and knocked on her door and said I had what she'd ordered. She looked me over so sharp I thought she was gonna say, 'Turn around a couple times,' but she didn't. Instead she told me to bring in the load, and then she said I should stay and

74

have a sample with her so she'd know she wasn't gonna get poisoned. She kinda kidded about it, but she meant it too."

"Isn't that what you told Howie, the lawyer, and me, was what happened on the last delivery? Are you mixed up?"

"No, I ain't mixed up, I ain't drunk and I ain't senile. She did the same thing the first time I saw her as the last. I just never thought about it before." He thought about it a moment longer and peered up at me, half-apologetic for his earlier annoyment. "That's funny, ain't it? She never asked me in any of the other times."

"Have you thought any about that last night, about what could've happened?"

"Sure. But my head gets all thick with it. It don't make sense that a man'd come in there and do that with me asleep right by."

"Try to think about it. It's a fairly big room and there's three couches in front of the fireplace. Two on each side, one across the middle, facing the hearth. Which one were you on?"

"The crossways one."

"Where was Kate sitting the last you remember?"

"Over to my right, on the couch facing the windows."

"At the end near you?"

"Uh-huh. She kept her drink on the side table next to the arm there."

"But she was strangled in the easy chair, west of the couches, facing the window, right?"

"That's where she was when the cops come, yeah."

"Uh-huh. And that was the only chair in the room facing away from the only door. It was behind the couch where you were sacked out so somebody could've come in, passed you and got to her without seeing you."

He thought a moment and shook his head. "He'd've seen me, unless it was a kid or a midget."

"Not if the room was dark. Did she have a fire going?"

"Naw. Too hot."

"Where'd you leave the truck?"

"By the back door. Them moon cans is heavy."

"And that back door's the only way into the cabin, right?"

"It's the only *door*."

That was a good point. The killer might have come in one of the bedroom windows on the west side. He could even have expected to find her in bed.

We sat a while, smoking and thinking. From his expression old Bos might've been sitting outside his cabin with a jug at his side, staring at the railroad tracks without a care in the world.

A guy in the next cell hawked and spat. I looked out through the door bars and saw another prisoner across the way, staring blankly at us. He looked so hung over it about gave me a headache.

I pumped Bos a little about Kate's asking him if he knew who his pa had been. That interested Kate more than seemed natural to Bos and she pressed him hard until he told her how his ma had claimed the old man was out seeking their fortune and would come back with money to take them to Missouri where they'd live in a fruit orchard and go outside every day to pick all the peaches and plums and berries they could eat.

"Ma was crazy about fruit," Boswell told me. "Loved blackberries. She thought Missouri was heaven 'cause it was loaded with fruit. Her favorite story was how Pa, when they lived back in Missouri, picked her a whole pailful of blackberries and hid 'em on top of the kitchen cabinet once when she was out hanging up a wash. When she come in she spotted it right off and asked him what was in that pail, and he wouldn't say and she had to get a chair and climb up to see. It was so high and so heavy she near dropped it and then she seen what it was and was so happy she bawled. She still bawled when she told me about it ten years later."

"What'd Kate say to all that?"

"She asked was he maybe dead. She figured Ma lied to me so I'd have something to look forward to. I told her that might've been so, but it wasn't. He run off with another woman. I didn't want to tell Kate that. I never told nobody that but you, Carl. You're the only fella I know that wouldn't figure somebody's bad because they done something wrong."

"You figure Kate was like a hanging judge?"

"She was awful critical. Not churchy. She could cuss real good and didn't go to Sunday meetings. But she was strong on the notion that there was good and there was bad people and they come in different lots without no mix."

"Did she talk about her father?"

"Well, she did say one thing kind of funny about that. When I told her I never knowed mine she said we had that in common—she'd never knowed hers either. Why'd she say a thing like that when she grew up right in her pa's house?"

"Lots of people live together and never know each other," I said. "Most marrieds don't know a goddamned thing about each other. The ones that do get divorced or kill each other."

He shook his head. "I don't believe that, Carl. I don't think you do neither."

"Maybe not."

"If you was as sour as you make out sometimes, you'd figure I choked Kate and stole her money."

"You got it all wrong, Bos. I know you didn't kill her because you haven't got the heft or ambition to knock off a woman who carries a blackjack. If you'd tried, she have busted your old head."

"No she wouldn't neither. I ain't as spry as you, but I can lift more gallons of whiskey than most my age and you know it."

"You can empty more, I'll admit that."

He puffed on his pipe and we were quiet a few minutes before I asked what Kate had said after telling him she hadn't known her father.

"I ain't too sure. I was getting kind of sleepy about then. It seems like she got a little excited, though. Said something about she was going to find out a lot of things real soon."

"Did you think she meant she was going to find them out the night you were there?"

"I dunno. I told you, I was sleepy."

"Drunk, more likely."

"I never get drunk, I just go to sleep."

"Uh-huh. Like Dan Boone never got lost, he just got confused for a few days. Okay. I'll come see you again soon. Meanwhile try to remember anything you can about what Kate said. It could maybe help."

Chapter IX

Monday Elihu came down sick and spent the night heaving and moaning. Ma comforted, fetched and hauled and generally tolerated his male weakness, and since I was around and had nothing more important to do than try to save my old friend's skin, she insisted I stick close and watch things until the old man recovered. I wasted the week watching the lobby, running errands and doing repair work in the apartments. Keeping the Wilcox Hotel in operation is like trying to move sand with a pitchfork. Everything's drying out, wearing down and breaking up, but the worst thing is that all that sweat, toil and frustration doesn't bring in enough money to keep even, let alone get ahead.

I did manage to enjoy old Eldridge, Pa's canary. He never gave a damn whether the old man was flat on his ass; the minute I took the cover off his cage he'd cut loose and sing like the sound of his song would guarantee a full seed tray, fresh water and protection against the winter. He was the happiest damned fool I ever saw.

When my nephew, Hank, was small, I caught him once standing on a chair, peeking inside the birdcage cover to see what Eldridge did in private. I don't know

what he expected but when I asked he said,
disgustedly, "He doesn't do anything but nothing."

By Saturday Elihu was up and in charge once more,
leaving me free. While I hadn't done half what he
thought I should during his vacation in bed, he felt
forced to be generous when I asked for his car, and that
night I set off for the lake in style.

Hollering Holly Horn's band was at the Wooden Palace by Lake Kampie, which meant there'd be
hayshakers, plow jockeys and small-town slickers in
from all points of the prairie. Holly's real name is
Hoerner, but he became Hollering Horn from the time a
local paper described his trumpet playing that way and
he adopted the title for his band. I hadn't seen him
since he'd been leading a four-piece combo with his old
man on the drums, so I decided to drift around and
hear how much better he was with eleven men backing
him up.

A breeze coming off the lake at dusk cooled the beach
strollers but couldn't penetrate into the Palace Bar
("The longest west of Chicago"). It had room enough
for half of South Dakota's citizenry to belly up and order beer, drink, talk, sweat and laugh. The joint reeked
of brew, tobacco smoke, fresh popcorn, a hint of sweep-
ing compound with maybe a whiff of prairie dust. The
smell of the lake never had a prayer.

Along the north wall kids stuck coins into pinball machines and shot toy pistols at little ball bearings or
snapped levers and tilted machines that threw off lights,
rang bells and clicked furiously while snapping out wild
scores. I greeted familiar characters and got the usual
questions about how come I was out of jail. A few
thumped my back and wanted to buy me a drink. These
were the ones that liked lies. I used to be good at what

the old-timey folks call tall tales, but when I started spelling out these stories I gave up most of the lying because it's so easy it can ruin you when you write. Talking's lots easier than writing and more fun, but it doesn't pay. Of course writing's never paid for me, but there's always that off-chance.

After a few beers I drifted up to the dance hall on the second floor at the east end of the Palace and edged around the dancing mob until I was close to the little bandstand. Windows had been opened on every side of the enormous room, but with a little breeze and some three hundred characters hugging and hopping, the air was thick as good potato soup and blamed near as hot. All the bandmen had shed their coats, and sweat poured from their foreheads and soaked their shirts. At every break the drummer swabbed his face and hands with a graying handkerchief that dripped. He was a young guy; obviously Hank had put his drumming pa out to pasture. This kid had an ungodly amount of energy and worked like he was convinced every piece of his equipment had to be tapped, pounded, brushed or slammed at least once a second or it'd feel neglected. It looked like he had four arms.

I worked up close to the stand and during their first break, got Holly's attention. He crouched above me and I took his sweating hand.

"Carl, you old jailbird," he grinned. "What do you think of my band?"

"It's great."

"You ain't seen nothing yet. We're the biggest thing in South Dakota, hell, the whole Midwest. We're gonna be the best anywhere. Pack 'em in like this everyplace we go. Jesus, ain't it grand? Hey, how long you been out?"

"So long I don't remember being in."

"Terrific. Still fighting?"

"Retired."

"I'll bet. Hey, what's this I hear about Boswell? They say he killed a woman—what kind of crap's that, anyway?"

"The worst kind. He was just handy and they're trying to hang it on him."

"Who's his lawyer?"

"Fella named Howie Collins."

"He any good?"

"He's all we got. He might be better if he thought he'd get paid."

A citizen came up to request a number and Horn grinned and nodded and was sweeter than honey and I suspected he was glad for the distraction so he wouldn't be expected to volunteer money for Boswell's lawyer. When the guy finally drifted off, Horn leaned closer.

"What's this lawyer doing for Bos?"

"He's letting me poke around to find out what might have happened."

"The old private-eye thing, huh? How you doing?"

"Mostly painting glass."

"You'd ought to talk with Fancy. She knew Kate Bonney a few years back."

"Fancy who?"

"My singer," he said, just as if he'd always had a canary with his outfit.

"She from around here?"

"Sure. Her old man's a doc at Pilgrim Hospital. Fancy worked there while Kate was still nursing. I heard her talking about it after she read about the murder. It shook Fancy up pretty good."

"Where's she now?"

"Be around any minute. I let her have the first half hour because she's eating dinner with her old man. Stick around, I'll introduce you."

I drifted off when he got up to revive the band.

A few moments later I spotted a slim girl making her way through the center of the dancers. Dark brown hair cut short made a cap on her small head. She had huge blue eyes with black lashes and thin eyebrows, rouged apple cheeks and stark red lipstick. She moved in dancing steps through the careening, hopping couples, made a brief face when bumped into and kept her balance and temper. She didn't bother to go around to the steps at the side of the bandstand but hitched up her skirt and with a combination hop and high step suddenly was standing beside Horn in his chair up front. He lifted his gaze from the music stand and frowned at her. A moment later she had him laughing.

Three minutes later Fancy moved up to the mike, and I learned she was a contralto. It didn't seem right for all that low, rich voice to come out of that frail girl in the white dress. She sang "Mood Indigo":

Woke up this morn', blues all 'round my head
    Woke up this mornin', wishin' I was dead

It was a goddamned crime, wasting a voice like that before a dance crowd and I was glad to see a few couples stop and stare at the beginning. Pretty soon, though, everyone went back to squeezing and sliding.

It was a long time before the next break came and I could go up for an introduction.

"Lady," I said, "what in the world are you doing with this hayshaker band?"

"Getting a start," she said, and grinned at Horn. Her eyes were bright with excitement. Her whole soul glowed.

Horn, who regularly referred to himself as a hick, didn't like it when anybody else made light of his outfit and impatiently butted in when I started to ask Fancy another question about her career.

"Carl's trying to dope out the murder of your friend, Kate What's-her-name."

Fancy's glow faded slowly as the remote murder moved in, evaporating her dream of fame and worshippers.

"Kate?" she said, staring at me.

I explained about Boswell.

Fancy looked at Horn.

"Boswell," said Horn, "was the janitor at Corden High. Hell of a great old guy, wouldn't, for Christ's sake, trap a rat. Too damned gentle. Carl here's trying to help him out."

"I understand you worked at the hospital with Kate," I said. "I'd like to talk with you about her."

She looked at me for the first time as something besides a fan and didn't seem too thrilled with the view.

"Did you know her?" she asked.

"No."

She looked over my head at the crowd. "I don't think there's much I could tell you."

"Talk to him during intermission later," said Horn. She looked at him, first in annoyance, then suddenly smiled and said sure, that'd be fine.

"You want a beer or something?" I asked as we walked toward the stairway through the happy mob.

"No. Let's go outside where we can breathe."

She moved through the crowd impatiently, squeezing between people, even shoving gently now and then. Guys would turn, glaring murder and then grin when they saw her. Even women managed to smile because she beamed at them so radiantly.

As soon as we escaped the crowd and were walking along the grassy area overlooking the beach, she slowed down and looked up, sighing.

"Crowds get me, all that smoke and noise."

"Aren't you in the wrong racket, then?"

"No. Everything costs, you know? And the minute I start to sing I don't care about anything else at all. It's the sitting and waiting, and not being able to *really* look at the people out there. If you let them meet your eyes they think you're trying to know them and they come up and want to take you over."

"I didn't notice anybody doing that."

"Well, you just betcha. As soon as I meet somebody's eyes I just lift my head and look over them. That cools men in a hurry. If you meet eyes and you're a girl and drop them, it's like an invitation. It's passive, you know?"

"You're not passive, huh?"

"No, I'm not."

She kept walking toward the water, then turned east and led me to the first dock below the residential area. It stood, like the others, stark and abandoned by the lake. She sat on the edge, flipped up her white dress, unfastened her garters and slipped her stockings off. She moved so quickly I barely glimpsed the slender white legs before the skirt was down again and she was up, walking through the sand toward the water. I slipped off my shoes and socks and followed her.

"When I was little," she said, "I used to sit on

docks and kick my feet in the water. I always liked the cool feel of it up to my knees. Beyond that it's almost always too cold."

"Your dad have a place on the lake?"

"Used to. It was about a quarter of a mile east of here. Not very big. I don't think Daddy ever liked it awfully well. He got it for me and my brother. He thought we should spend our summers at the lake. As soon as Billy went off to medical school, Daddy sold the cabin."

"Weren't you going to be a nurse once?"

"No. I wasn't going to be anything but maybe a doctor. I worked one summer at the hospital, to see what it'd be like, and I found out I'd never want to be in a place like that for the rest of my life. I don't like people in pain and dependent. I mean, I'm sympathetic and all that. I feel sorry, you know? But I don't feel like I can *really* help them and if you can't, why hang around and feel miserable yourself?"

"My sentiments, exactly."

She faced me. "You understand that, no kidding?"

"Hell, yes."

She turned and walked on. "Daddy couldn't at all. Kate could. Kate told me she had this mixed-up feeling about invalids. She liked them dependent, but she hated for them to expect too much from her."

"Was she the one that decided you against doctoring?"

"*I* decided. Why should I be giving people enemas, shots and all that when I can make them happy by singing and have them love me for it?"

"I imagine your old man figures taking care of the sick is a higher calling."

"You can darned bet, even though he does make fun

of himself sometimes—says he's only a white-coated mechanic. I just figure two medics in the family is enough. They can have it, and men are the only ones that really can. I don't want any part of fighting all the guys, the way Kate did."

"You always wanted to be a singer?"

"All my life. From the first time I sang a solo in church I knew that was what I was going to do when I grew up. When you sing and people like it, their eyes get a special glow. You had it when you came up to the stand. It was so light I didn't really see your face, just the expression and the shine in your eyes."

I suspected she had caught a reflection, since I'm hardly the glowing kind, but she was so happy I hadn't the heart to deflate her.

"It's quite a talent. If you can stick out the crowds and smoke, I guess you'll go as far as you like."

She shook her head solemnly. "Nobody goes that far. But I'm going to try."

We were in the water up to our ankles and she began walking back west, taking small steps with each foot placed carefully in front of the other as she swung her shoulders gently. I sloggged along beside her, trying to avoid any splashing that'd wet her skirt.

"So you only knew Kate while you were at the hospital. What—three months?"

"I'd met her before that at the lake. Her cabin was fairly close to ours."

"Were you ever in it?"

"Sure. Kids always went over to Kate's. She gave us cookies and milk, pop—even hotdogs if you stuck around. Sometimes on a Friday night she'd build a fire down on the beach and a whole gang would show up to tell stories and sing. Kate played a little ukelele."

"How'd she manage that with two fingertips missing?"

"Well, she didn't really play much more than chords. Before I realized her handicap I used to ask her to play numbers like 'The Gallant Major' and 'Springtime in the Rockies' and 'My Blue Heaven,' and she'd just say she didn't know them. But if I'd sing the words she'd play chords so we could sing."

"It sounds like you knew her pretty well."

"Yes, I lied before. I didn't think I wanted to talk about her so soon after she . . . died. She was very special to me for a while there. I owed her a lot. She told me I could be as good as Connie Boswell. Nobody else ever encouraged me like that. Daddy didn't say it was a stupid notion, he just pulled a mouth when anything was said about me being a singer, and could tell he thought it was a juvenile phase I had to go through. I guess that was even worse than if he'd gotten mad or insisted I go to medical school. I decided to work at the hospital just to please him, and for the first month he was so happy I felt good about it because he's really an awfully nice person—everybody wants to please him."

"How about Kate?"

"Even she did. But when I came to the hospital and she saw I was doing it just to please him, she told me it was fine to be nice to your parents, but it was idiotic to live your life for them. I think she was right. Don't you?"

"Damn right."

She reached over and grasped my wrist. "You're very understanding; I like you. I didn't think I would at first, after I looked at you when we'd been talking a while. How come you don't think like other older people?"

"Probably because I'm not as old as I look."

"Go on. You're over thirty, aren't you?"

"That's not as old as it looks to you. Hell, it's no more than eight or so years ahead of you."

"It's forever ahead of me. Even next year's forever away. Anyway, don't start getting touchy. I don't really think you look so old, but you are mature and still very unstuffy. I talk too much about me and you listen like you were interested. You aren't going to make a pass, are you?"

"I don't think so. I'd like to, but I'd guess you get so many it'd be tiresome, especially coming from an old man."

She laughed. "You're working on me, now. Listen, I've got to get back. Old Horn'll really howl if I'm late. We'll talk later, okay?"

"No more lies?"

"Not hardly any."

When we'd walked as far as the grass she stopped to put her stockings back on. She did it with marvelous balance and grace, standing on one leg at a time. It was a much better show than the removal because it took a little longer, but it still went too fast. She turned her back when everything was hitched up and asked if her seams were straight.

"Perfect," I said.

She took my arm for the rest of the walk and I'll admit it gave me a kick to see the look of amazement on guys we passed when they glommed my partner.

The sax man and the drummer glared at me when I delivered Fancy to the bandstand, but Horn just nodded like a kindly father. They were already playing and the dance floor was filled with tight couples and sweaty romance. Fancy climbed up and looked over the crowd and her face glowed because soon she'd be singing.

Chapter X

I leaned against the east wall and smoked while watching the guys prowl and the girls wait. Guys never sit down at a dance unless they find an empty chair beside a girl they want to hustle. Girls never stand except when they've accepted an offer and get up to dance.

"What's the matter," asked a voice at my shoulder, "you too shy to ask a girl out on the floor?"

I turned and found myself looking at Polly Erickson. It took a second to realize this was the barefooted kid I'd seen outside Kate's cabin. She was all dressed up in pale green and high heels. Her freckles were almost hidden under powder and she was wearing too much lipstick, but the green eyes were bright and honest.

"The fact is," I told her, "I'm not that light-footed."

"You think I'm too young."

"Not for dancing," I said and we moved out into the mob.

It was a slow enough number for me to move with, and I used my walk step, which when somebody like my nephew Hank does it looks like the ballroom stuff but with me is just walking.

"What's happening?" asked Polly.

"Well, so far I haven't stepped on my partner's feet."

"I mean about Kate's murder."

"Oh. Not much. I've talked with some people. They all seemed to have known a different Kate."

"What about Francis Franklin, which one did she know?"

I looked down at her with my eyebrows up and she tilted her head toward the bandstand. "The singer, calls herself Fancy."

"I didn't know—well, she knew her a long while back. We've just started talking, but she liked Kate. I don't know if she can tell me anything helpful."

"You like her looks?"

"Why not?"

"She's loaded with makeup. A person can't really tell what she looks like under all that."

"She probably looks about the same—except maybe with freckles, like others I know."

"I haven't got all that rouge on."

"You look just fine, better than fine, easily as good as Fancy. But she does sing good, doesn't she?"

"She sounds like a man."

"You know her?" I asked. The antagonism seemed too strong for impersonal jealousy.

"Never saw her before you walked in with her hanging on your arm."

"I didn't see you."

"You were too busy looking smug."

"That takes a lot of my attention," I admitted.

"Did you talk to the Ryders?"

"Twice. At least to her."

"I guess you like talking to women."

"Only when they don't jump on me. Come on, get

that burr out from under the saddle and grin. You look like a Methodist deacon."

"She's too tall for you."

"You're probably right. And her boyfriend's too fat for her. There's blamed few perfect matches in this world—except maybe you and me."

"You're making fun," she said, but I got the grin I was looking for.

As I walked her toward the chairs after the dance ended, we were intercepted by a nervous young man who reached cautiously for her arm and stammered something about having lost her.

"I saw Carl," she said, rather loftily. "He's an old friend."

The boy looked at me with pale blue eyes under blond brows. Fine, short hair gave his skull a fuzzy look.

"Hi," he said. "I'm Peter."

He looked like a guy who'd be robbed to pay Paul. I said hi and accepted the slender hand pushed toward me. He expected me to try and crush it and shoved his palm in tight to protect his fingers. When I didn't squeeze he gave me a tentative smile.

"Polly and I are in the same class at school," he told me. "I took her to the prom."

"You must've been a fine-looking couple."

"Carl's investigating a murder," said Polly. "He's not interested in our history."

Peter's eyes fastened on me.

"The Kate Bonney murder?"

"Everybody seems to have heard of it."

"We don't get a lot of murders around here," he said.

"Sometimes I think there are more than people realize."

"Will you be coming around to the cabin again?" Polly asked.

"I doubt it. The Frenches don't seem to know much they want to tell me."

"Well, you'll have to work on them."

Peter suggested they dance and she ignored him.

"You can't just let people not talk," she told me. "You have to keep after them."

"I never thought of it that way," I said, and smiled so it wouldn't seem too sarcastic.

"The trouble is, you're too easygoing. If you're going to be a private detective you have to be very persistent."

"I'm not a private eye. I'm just a guy trying to help out a friend in trouble."

"Well, you shouldn't have to be paid to work hard."

"Is that advice from your father—or did you read it in a book?"

She flushed, turned to Peter and said, "Let's dance."

"Good-bye, sir," said Peter, and followed after her.

I told myself it was better to be called "sir" than "pop," but it didn't ease the irritation much, and I decided to go outside for some fresh air.

On the beach the wind had died, leaving a threatening silence all around. I strolled along the shore, looking north over the silent water, and approached the point where the high bluff still collapsed, bit by bit, when the actions of freeze and thaw cracked boulders loose and sent them crashing through the broken trees to what was once water and now was sand. The rocks were only a few yards ahead when I heard footsteps in the sand behind me. I turned as a new breeze came to life, whispering through the trees nearby.

There were two of them. They walked easy, one just behind and to the right of the other, like men with a purpose but nothing urgent.

I turned, went on toward the rocks, hopped a small one, then a larger, stopped on a fine, flat-topped boulder and turned around. The men came on, separating slightly. The wind became a little stronger, rustling cottonwood leaves overhead. I suddenly realized there were no stars. It surprised me because I always look up when I go outside and I couldn't think why I had not before—or why I did now.

The man in the lead stopped below my perch.

"Your name Wilcox?" It was meant, I guessed, to be a question, but it came out as a statement, almost an indictment.

"That's part of it," I confessed.

"Come on down, I want to talk to you."

His partner moved casually to my left. I doubted he could scramble up to my level from there but kept my eye on him in case he carried something that'd be damaging from a distance.

"You can talk to me from there," I said.

"It's nothing we can holler about."

"I believe you, but I hear good. Fire away."

"What're you scared of? I heard you had guts."

"Not me, you got the wrong Wilcox. I shy from pairs on the beach that follow me on dark and stormy nights."

"I'll come up there."

"You do and you won't stay."

His friend moved around in back of me. It was hard to figure what he had in mind and it made me as nervous as he planned it should.

The first man came up on the nearest rock toward

him, then the next. I moved to meet him. He looked big and sure as a twice-elected politician.

I suppose I should be ashamed to admit I sometimes fight with my feet, but when a man's no bigger than me and can't stand guns, he needs all he's got to keep even in this world.

I feinted a right kick and as he ducked and raised his arm to catch my leg I caught him a thumping smack with my left foot that knocked him spinning. He hit the sand head first and rolled flat on his back. His partner found a hold in the rock behind me and was up in a crouch by the time I swung around to face him. He feinted a left twice, both snake-quick, and I shuffled right, left, tried a feint of my own and snapped it back as he took a pass at my fist. A sharp pain streaked across my big left knuckle and I realized he was using a knife.

That changed the whole dance, of course. I'd known from his first move he was fast, but I could see he wasn't any bigger than me and not enough smaller to have a leverage advantage so I was comfortable. But the knife made everything different. You don't block or slip a blade without cost if the man using it knows what he's doing and this bastard did. He kept his left ahead of the knife hand and rocked his crouching body back and forth in uneven motion as he took tiny forward steps while keeping his feet well spread. Since my first jump back had used up my retreating territory and there was no place for side movement, my only direction was forward or down. I made a move as if to turn and jump, wheeled, dropped both hands to the rock and threw my right foot at him. He caught it flush on the mouth. The impact jerked an agonized grunt from him at the same time a flame cut across my lower thigh and the next moment he was thudding to the ground.

I stood up, looking for the big guy and couldn't find him. The second was sprawled on the sand, motionless. I checked my leg and found a shallow, inch-and-a-half cut a little above the knee. My pants were cut bad enough to flap. I sucked my bleeding knuckle a moment, then climbed down from the rock, took another look around and hiked toward the pavilion.

Lou Corsi was doing security duty and agreed to come back and take a look when I told him there was a man hurt on the beach. Lou's a big, not too bright farmboy who was too smart to stay on his pa's starving farm and had moved into town where he got a job as a cop. He'd been doing special duty at the dance hall for over five years and more than once had broken up fights I'd either been in or had managed to start between others. He wasn't a really lazy man so he didn't resent the fact I made his evenings a little more interesting. We got along fine.

"This some kid interested in your woman?" he asked as we crunched along the beach.

"No," I said, and told him what'd happened.

The beach area around the rocks was deserted when we arrived. Lou made some cracks about me seeing pink hoodlums but turned on his flash and flicked it over the sand around the rocks where I'd entertained the pair. We found signs of blood about two yards from the big rock.

"I'd guess that's where the guy with the knife landed," I told Lou.

"You figure you kicked him in the mouth?"

"That's right. I was aiming for his jaw, but he scrunched down a couple inches."

"You're a menace," said Lou.

"What about those two palookas?"

"Babes in the wood. Anybody dumb enough to jump you in the dark shouldn't be let out of the nursery. Did the big guy have a knife or anything?"

"I don't know, we never got formally acquainted."

"We'd ought to find loose teeth around if you really caught him in the kisser," he said, and brought the light close to the sand. "Probably shucked 'em like corn kernels."

He wanted a description of the guys, but since it'd been so dark I couldn't offer him much. I finally told him I wanted to get back to the dance before it ended.

"Ah," he said wisely, "you got a heavy date with that singer chick, huh?"

"We're gonna talk, yeah."

"Uh-huh. I know your kind of talk. In this case I'll bet you never make it. That kid's saving herself for movie stars."

I didn't pick up on that and he drifted back toward the bar, saying he'd ask around to see if he could pick up a lead on my beach buddies.

The crowd had thinned a little by the time Horn's band played "Good Night Ladies," but the hall was a long ways from deserted and several jerks hung around the bandstand while the guys were gathering their music and casing their instruments. Three guys and a girl kept talking to Fancy, and even more annoying, she kept talking to them. I finally moved close and said, "Hey!"

She ignored me. One of the three guys gave me a scowl, nudged his friend and they both gave me the evil eye. I handed it back and even took a step forward before Fancy suddenly told the two still facing her that she had to go and stepped over to where she could reach down for my hand.

"Don't start anything," she whispered in a mad tone. "I don't even talk to guys that fight—"

"Who's starting anything?" I demanded as we walked toward the stairs.

"You were ready to. You looked murder at those boys because I didn't jump the moment you spoke."

"They were giving me dirty looks."

"Well, that's certainly a great reason to start a fight."

"The only fight I know about is one you're trying to start with me right now. What's happened to make you so edgy?"

"I'm not edgy, and I'm not looking for a fight. Do you want to talk or don't you?"

"Hell, yes, but—"

"Then we'll go where we can have some coffee and quiet, okay?"

I said that was great and off we hiked to her Ford which was parked under a cottonwood at the edge of the lot. Before getting in she stopped and turned to me.

"Now, there's got to be an understanding. No passes, no pawing—nothing like that. Is it agreed?"

"I won't if you don't."

She made a noise that I'd call a snort if she weren't so ladylike, and the next moment she was wheeling us out of the lot.

"Listen," I said. "Has somebody been talking to you about me?"

"Why'd anybody talk to me about you?"

"Because that band is nuts about you and none of them love me, and your whole attitude has changed since less than two hours ago. Something happened."

"There was some talk," she admitted. She spoke with her eyes on the road and tilted her head slightly my way. "The fellows are very protective. They worry about me."

"Well, they probably didn't say anything about me that wasn't at least half true."

"I don't want to hear about it. We're going to talk about Kate and that's all we have to cover, right?"

She was right, of course, but I'd really enjoyed it earlier when she'd treated me like a favorite uncle, and the hostility twisted my thoughts from inquiry to defense, so the whole mission was all warped out of shape and we rode in silence. I didn't even wonder for a while where the hell she could be taking us after midnight on a Saturday morning.

Chapter XI

Suddenly we were in the rich part of Aquatown and Fancy turned the Ford up a side drive and parked under a small roof without walls. I sat gawking as she climbed out and then made a scramble to open the door and come around the car to join her. She'd gone up two steps and was opening the screen by the time I caught up.

"What the hell?"

"This is my father's house. There's no place decent open this late. I'll make us coffee and we can talk in the kitchen. Just don't make any noise to wake him. Follow me."

That wasn't as easy as she made it sound since she turned on no lights, but I trailed along and soon we were in a large kitchen which she brought into partial view by lighting a gas lamp on the north wall. Like the kitchen at the hotel, this one had a huge black wood-stove off center near the west wall. Beside it was a spindly legged gas stove with a white, waist-level oven. Long counters flanked the east entrance and a solid oak table owned the center of the room. The floor was all polished hardwood wideboards.

"You must have servants," I said.

"There's a hired girl," said Fancy. She lifted a percolater from the gas stove, filled it at the sink to my right and after lighting the gas with a wooden match from a wall holder, put the pot over the blue flame.

I parked on a heavy wooden chair beside the big table and watched as she took a coffee can from one of the endless counters and measured coffee into the percolator seive.

"Doesn't the doctor believe in electricity?" I asked.

"We have it. He put it in a couple years ago, but he never took the gas jets out and I like the light they give—at least out here. I've always loved the kitchen. I don't want it different from the way it looked when I was little."

She perched on the chair edge across from me while the coffee water was heating, and I asked her why she'd really lied about knowing Kate, and she insisted it was for the reason she'd first given me.

"Was she a lesbian?"

She leaned forward, putting her elbows on the table as she cupped her chin.

"A lot of people said so. All I know is she never·tried to do anything to me. I suspect Daddy has other notions or thought that'd change. I don't really know. Kate had very strong ideas about doing things properly most of the time. I mean, she'd absolutely hate to have anybody think she was a tacky person. She wanted community respect. That may sound foolish, knowing she drank bootleg booze and lots of times swore like a man. But she couldn't stand the notion of being looked down on or condescended to. She knew people would be contemptuous if they thought or could prove she was something . . . strange. She wouldn't mind being considered wicked or even cruel—but never tasteless. Do you understand what I'm trying to say?"

I nodded solemnly and told her I thought the coffee

water was about ready to boil. She hopped up, swiftly lowered the flame and stood watching as the water began shooting up and splashing brown against the glass top.

"Was Kate really so unpopular with the doctors?" I asked.

"And how. They were all used to having nurses kiss their feet and jump like trained poodles at every word. Believe me, when Kate let them know about their mistakes or made suggestions about *any*thing, they just absolutely *froze*. But she had friends, too. A couple of the younger guys and even one or two older ones, the smart people."

She sat down again, glanced at her wristwatch and looked back at the coffee while she talked.

"So why'd your dad want her out of the hospital?"

"Well, Kate really *did* cause a lot of fuss. There was a group of doctors who called themselves the 'Let's Kill Kate Klan,' and they'd gather and mutter about her. And then there was a group of nurses that defended her and it made for a very strange atmosphere in a hospital. One day Daddy asked me all about the big to-do and I was dumb enough to tell him because I thought it was all pretty funny. I guess he didn't. Kate never blamed me, but I blamed myself. I should have realized—"

A toilet flushed upstairs and Fancy frowned.

"Your old man?" I asked. She nodded. "How's he going to feel about you bringing me here?"

"He won't fuss. I just hope wè didn't wake him. He has trouble sleeping—"

We heard the stairs creak and waited in silence until a small ghost in a black robe and brown slippers appeared in the doorway. A shock of white hair topped a pale, thin face with hollow cheeks, sympathetic eyes and a wide mouth that drooped at the corners.

His brows lifted a fraction as he took me in.

"Daddy, this is Carl Wilcox."

He frowned thoughtfully. "The man who called me today?"

"Right," I said, and stood up.

His slipper heels dragged as he came forward into the dim gaslight. There was nothing ghostly about the sharp eyes as he examined me, and I realized he was not as old as the white hair and robe made me think at first glance.

Fancy began explaining where we had met and what I was doing. She talked fast, leaning over the kitchen table, but her father's eyes stayed on me.

"Sit down," he told me, interrupting her, and we took places across from each other. Fancy's flow of gab dried up. She went over to the stove, turned off the heat, brought back the coffee pot, realized she didn't have a cup for her father, put the pot back, got a cup and finally poured for all of us.

"Is someone paying you for this investigation?" he asked after tasting the hot coffee.

"No, but I'm open to offers."

He moved his cup handle, turning it gently back and forth. "You're just coming to the aid of a friend?"

"Giving it a try."

"Full time?"

"I don't have a regular job, if that's what you're asking."

"How do you live?"

"Mostly on the edge, Doc."

He ran thin fingers through his tousled hair, brought the hand down to the table and lifted the coffee cup to his mouth for a cautious drink.

"Whose idea was it to come here?" he asked Fancy.

"Mine," she said. "There wasn't anyplace else to talk where we could get coffee."

"Remarkable," said Doctor Franklin as he leaned back and stared at me. "Tell me about your friend."

I did.

He listened without comment, finally put his elbows on the table and tilted his head. "Boswell hardly sounds like a good murder suspect. Did you know that Kate Bonney's father committed suicide?"

I nodded.

"It was right after the Crash. Some people around here said he couldn't face people who'd lost their savings in his bank. Others hinted the bank was already bankrupt before the Crash, that he'd removed almost all of its assets by the close of twenty-eight, maybe sooner. Did you ever hear any of that?"

"Yeah."

"It was a popular topic of conversation in this area for a long time. As far as I know, no one ever found a trace of the money. Some speculated that Timmerman anticipated the Crash and embezzled the cash on hand. If so, why'd he kill himself when the Crash occurred and his theft might never have been discovered?"

"He probably figured people'd be digging to find goats and he'd get nailed," I said. "But more likely he was milking the bank and hadn't figured on the general foldup. Probably panicked when it came."

"Well, we'll never know, will we? I raised the subject because there were lots of people who thought Kate had money her father left secretly. They particularly suspected that when she left the hospital and never looked for work again. It'll be interesting to see what sort of money she actually had—and who she left it to."

"What happened to Kate's mother?"

"She died very shortly after the daughter's finger accident. Died in her sleep, I understand. Doctor Gloecker was the physician. I never knew him very well; he was an old man. If I remember correctly, he died about five or six years ago."

"How'd Kate feel about her mother?"

He shrugged. Fancy said they were quite close.

"At least that's how Kate talked," said Fancy. "She told me her mother was crazy about fairy tales and romances and read them to her."

When I started to roll a cigaret, the Doc asked me how I'd cut my hand.

"Accident," I said.

"Have you washed it?"

"Sucked it a little."

"What about the cut on your leg—did you suck that clean?"

I stared at him. "Don't tell me. You got a call from Lou Corsi?"

"No, from his employer."

"You get a complete line on everything that goes on, eh, Doc?"

"I have a lot of friends," he granted. "There was some concern about your interest in Fancy."

"Were the guys on the beach friends of yours?"

He smiled. "Not that I know of. Of course they may have thought they were."

"It must be nice to have so much influence."

"Let's not belabor a feeble joke. Now, let me have a look at that leg wound."

I said why not and at his suggestion, dropped my pants. I've never been shy and I figured Fancy had seen lots more during her summer in the hospital. He got her to bring a soapy cloth and cleaned me up some, then sent her after bandaging stuff.

"Do you think those men were trying to kill you?" he asked. His tone was purely curious.

"Hard to say. I think by the time the second one got close he meant business. Guys with knives usually do."

"An old grudge? Or someone afraid?"

"You got me. From all I've dug up so far I don't know what the hell anybody'd be afraid of."

"I've a feeling that people who kill don't need logical reasons. The ones who hire killers may be different, but I doubt it."

"So you had nothing to do with it, huh?"

"Not a thing." He was very cheerful about it.

"Why'd Kate leave the hospital?"

"Because it was the wise thing to do, for everyone concerned."

"Why?"

"She wasn't happy there. She upset her superiors, caused dissension—"

"That made some people madder than hell, didn't it?"

"Something like that."

"Did she burn you, Doc?"

"No. She was never insubordinate with me. As far as my experience went, she was efficient, capable and highly intelligent. Unfortunately she wasn't diplomatic and she couldn't keep still. When you work in a hospital, there are times when you must be both."

"So you just had a little chat with her and she agreed to quit. That's all there was to it?'"

"Essentially. She didn't agree at that very moment. I suggested she think it over and she said she would. She was very rational about the matter. And when she reached her decision, she told me without recriminations."

"Did the subject of her lesbianism come up during your little chat?"

Just then Fancy returned with cotton, gauze and tape and for a few moments nobody said anything as he bandaged my cut.

"What?" I said. "No stitches?"

"You only need them in your pants."

I accepted Fancy's offer of more coffee, rolled another cigaret and squinted through the lifting smoke at Dr. Franklin.

"What about that last question, Doc?"

"The subject never came up."

"Fancy never got mentioned, huh?"

"Certainly not."

Fancy frowned and lifted her chin.

"Why'd you ask that? What was the question before I came in?"

Dr. Franklin watched me. I couldn't tell if he was angry, worried or just interested.

"I asked him if Kate's lesbianism came up at the time he was telling her she should leave the hospital."

Fancy turned to stare at her father. He still watched me.

"If Kate upset the doctors," I said, "I'm not about to believe at least one of them didn't tell you they figured she was a lesbian, and probably hinted she was a little too interested in your kid."

"Nobody'd say anything like that to Daddy," said Fancy. "He just doesn't hear gossip so the people don't talk that way to him."

"Let me level, Doc," I said. "Are you trying to make me believe that not one of those guys that hated Kate, ever came around to warn you that Fancy might get seduced?"

He sighed and looked fondly at his daughter.

"All right, yes, I was approached on the subject. A delegation came to see me after making an appointment. They began with talk about Nurse Bonney's insubordinate attitudes, her bad influence on co-workers. They said she was a rebel and troublemaker. When that didn't appear to impress me they began making implications about her sexual preferences. They saved Fancy for last."

"Is that why you asked her to resign?" I asked.

"It was not out of concern for Fancy. I've been all too aware of her fondness for boys—and men—to be concerned about deviations. What impressed me was that Kate had so upset the staff they felt compelled to descend that far to get her removed. I put it all to Nurse Bonney just that day and eventually she agreed. I don't think she was particularly upset about leaving. What made her reluctant was to see them win over her."

"Did you ever see her again?'"

"No."

I butted my cigaret out in an ashtray Fancy put beside me and squinted at him.

"One more question. You seem to've been the only man in the place that Kate had any respect for. Did anybody ever hint they thought you and she were more than, well, professionally interested'?"

He laughed shortly, then glanced at Fancy. "*I* never heard such a thing. Did you?"

Fancy shook her head and stared into her coffee cup.

"Did Kate ever make a pass at you?" I asked her.

Her head jerked and she stared at me.

"What do you mean?"

"You know what I mean."

"Well, she touched me a few times. On the arm and the shoulder. That's all. She never went beyond that and she never asked me to meet her outside the hospital. I don't remember that she did that with anybody. I mean, I saw lots of the nurses that you could tell were very close friends and all that, like girls always are, but Kate didn't have any favorites. I think what those doctors said to Daddy was just out of spite."

We were silent while Fancy got up and poured more coffee. Then Doc Franklin leaned forward, rested his elbows on the table and stared at me as if I were a patient with a serious but not quite fatal ailment.

"I don't think you're going to find any connection between Kate's death and the hospital. It's more likely she was killed by a relative or a lover. And I agree with your conviction that it couldn't have been your friend, nor is it likely a casual thief was the killer. People like that are crude and panicky. They use clubs, guns or knives, not a strangler's cord. At least not in this country."

"If you were going to kill someone, how'd you do it?"

His white eyebrows went up and he gave me a somewhat confused smile. "I've no idea. It's not a thing I've ever considered."

"Consider it."

"I can't. It's too alien to my whole thought processes. My mind rejects the idea absolutely." His smile became more relaxed. "Now, doesn't that make me the prime suspect? The man who couldn't possibly be guilty?"

"Seems like. But I'll have to come up with a recent motive. How about it, Fancy. Had you seen Kate lately?"

She shook her head. "Not since she left the hospital."

Dr. Franklin pushed his coffee cup toward the table center and stood up. I stood too and was surprised to find how small he was. Somehow, when we talked at the table, he grew bigger.

"Well, this has been very interesting. I wish you luck, Mr. Wilcox, both in your investigation and your ride back with Fancy. She's a skillful, but I'm afraid reckless, driver. Good night."

When he was gone Fancy rinsed off cups and tidied up the kitchen.

"Do you know if Kate ever saw any other people she'd been friends with at the hospital once she quit?" I asked.

"I don't think so. Some I knew even mentioned it. She'd been so much of a—well, almost mother for a while—everyone depended on her so and they thought she'd keep in touch. Mostly they finally decided that she'd been more hurt than she'd admit and she couldn't handle the humiliation of anything like trying to hang on, you know?"

I nodded.

She picked up her small purse and for a moment held it beneath her breast while she stared at the table. Then she looked at me.

"Do you think Daddy made Kate quit because of me?"

"It doesn't make any difference now, does it?"

"It shouldn't, but, yes, it does."

"Why?"

"Well, first it'd mean he's not really quite all I've thought. I mean, he shouldn't have done a thing like that to Kate for personal reasons. And second, it would mean he didn't have much faith in me."

"Does that make you mad?"

"No. It makes me feel guilty."

Chapter XII

It was after two when Fancy dropped me off beside my old man's Dodge near the Palace. Over-hanging trees made the area darker than a witch's left teat, and by the time I'd fumbled around and got the key into the switch, her car was disappearing beyond the first bend. I hit the starter and was a little surprised when the engine turned over and wondered for a second why that didn't seem perfectly normal.

Driving down the long hill east of Bender's Slough, about two miles from the Palace, I remembered a few years earlier, when my old man hit a jackknifed truck at that hill bottom. The accident nearly killed both Ma and Pa and finished his real manhood. Every time I drove that hill I remembered the Chicago hoodlum who'd arranged the crackup and felt good about the fact I'd beaten the son-of-a-bitch.

The slough spreads for over a quarter of a mile on each side of the road, and once, when South Dakota knew rain, it had been a shallow lake stretching north and south nearly two miles long and half a mile wide. Now it was a shrinking bog filled with weeds, cattails and mudhens. The graveled highway ran through its

center with wooden posts and cables set up to keep
drunks from running into the muck.

Just before I reached the causeway a flash of light reflected in the rearview mirrow and I glanced up to see
headlights dip as a car or truck started down behind me,
moving fast.

I glanced at the gas gauge. It registered empty.

Since I'd left Corden in the morning with a full tank,
it didn't take any Sherlock to figure out somebody'd si-
phoned off most of it while I was with Fancy. And the
next conclusion was that somebody planned for me to
run out of gas in the prairie between the lake and
Corden. They couldn't have picked a better spot than
the middle of that slough.

I slammed on the brakes, felt the rear end start a
right swing, turned with it, tapped the gas pedal, hit the
brake again and wound up sliding in a cloud of dust and
gravel over the left bank. I missed the first barrier post
by half a mustache hair and landed in the slough with a
splash and gurgle.

Before the Dodge stopped moving I was out the door
and into the mire. Three sloshing strides brought me to
firm ground and I lit out, heading south.

I'm too damned bowlegged for first-class sprinting
and too lazy for marathon stuff, but under the circum-
stances covering lots of territory in the shortest time had
all the appeal of a night in the sack with a gorgeous
woman, since I figured whoever had gone to so much
trouble for a private chat probably was buddies with the
beach boys I'd entertained earlier in the evening.

I raced along the slough's edge at first, but after
stepping into boggy spots and stumbling twice, I began
angling uphill. A glance back assured me my lead was

safe against anything but a sniper's rifle so I started
climbing steeper. Never make it easy for people chasing
you.

The backward peek didn't tell me much. The sky was
moonless and bright-starred. All I could be sure of was
my hunters had been traveling in a truck, a fairly big one
with an almost square box rear.

When I pulled up at the crest of a low section of hills
bordering the slough's east end, I felt pretty satisfied
with myself. It didn't seem likely anyone was going to
catch up. Then the earth a foot from my right shoe exploded, I felt a sharp stinging up my right shin and immediately a rifle shot echoed across the valley.

I jumped a yard in the air and landed in a running
crouch so low my hands brushed the grass as I
zigzagged like a maniac. Considering the dark and the
distance, the shooter was either damned good or ungodly lucky and either way it meant bad news for me. The
second and third shots weren't quite so close, but I
heard them strike and ricochet near enough. I pounded
on like a stampeded steer until I stepped into an unseen
hollow, did a tumble and rolled for six yards. This time,
probably because I was rolling, I didn't hear lead hit
the earth, but a yell following the rifle shot told me the
gunner thought he'd scored a bulls-eye. The spill caused
enough sore spots to make me think he might be right,
and for a second I lay still, thinking about it. When I
tried moving, all parts responded so I rolled to all fours
and scrambled over the hill crest. The moment I
reached a low spot I straightened up and took off
again.

It was mostly grazed land from there on, all small
hills and cowpies. I kept to the low ground, trotting

steadily and worked east, back toward town.

Eventually I reached a fence before a graveled road and crouched down, looked both ways, checked behind me and peered ahead. Beyond the far ditch a cornfield rippled in the prairie wind. I flattened out, shoved up the lowest barbed wire strand and rolled under. Two long steps took me into the shallow ditch and again I looked all around, listening so hard it made my head ache, but there was no sound but the wind. I couldn't even hear the slough's croaking frogs any more.

About halfway across the road I heard an engine and over the hill to my left came a truck with its lights out. Two jumps put me across the road and ditch, then I got my hand on the first fence post, vaulted over and whish—I was in the corn.

Naturally, since I wanted to head east, the corn was planted in rows running north by south. Also it'd've been handy if the corn had been head high, but it came only to my shoulders and the wind pushed the tops even lower. I charged ahead, crouching like a man with a gut ache, and kept knocking over stalks and stumbling on mounds. The truck came along the road. I could see the rear-end box, high and white against the star-flecked sky. He still hadn't turned on his lights. By the time I'd run half a block into the field the truck was even with me on the road and it stopped.

I quit charging against the rows, wheeled to the east and galloped down the open row. The level path was a great relief but I still had a problem trying to make good time while running bent over like a weasel in a prairie dog tunnel.

After about a month of that I came to a whoa and squatted to listen. The truck was moving, I heard the whine of the reverse gear, so evidently they'd seen or heard which way I was headed.

Were they both in the truck? Were there more than two guys?

I raised my head not quite clear of the cornstalks and stared around. A man was moving into the cornfield, towering above it, carrying a rifle at high port. He was alone. The truck kept moving backward, not parallel with me yet but moving as fast as I'd been running.

I ducked down, wriggled through about six rows of corn to the west, then moved easy on hands and knees back toward the rifleman. When I could hear him clearly I halted again, crouching low but keeping my feet under me. If he came close enough and passed, I'd jump him. The problem was I'd been running half the night and for the past hour I'd been in a crouch, which cramped my legs. I wasn't sure I had enough spring to make a good jump, let alone the heft to handle the bastard when I landed. He didn't look much bigger than God.

He passed about three rows to my left. That was two rows too many to jump, even if I'd felt up to it, and I let him go his way, thinking that some day I'd meet him when he didn't have a cannon, and then maybe we'd see how handy he was. I thought about it with relish because the fact is I dearly despise being chased around like a poor-assed jackrabbit.

As I was trying to decide whether to trail this big bastard or move south, a light flared from the truck. I ducked tight and held still for several seconds. The rifleman moved on; I could hear the corn leaves rustle against his clothes. Slowly I raised up. The truck driver was standing on the rear box, pointing a big flashlight at

the field and moving it slowly back and forth before the
rifleman. Suddenly it swung my way and I went flatter
than a run-over snake.

I scratched the notion of following the hunter.

A long, long time later the truck engine started again.
When it moved off north and faded away, I held still as
long as I could and then raised up enough to gawk
around. There was nothing in sight but swaying corn,
dark hills and starry sky.

I sat down, straightened out my aching legs, lowered
my shoulders, felt the dry earth against my back—and
went to sleep.

Chapter XIII

Crows woke me. I opened my eyes to the sky all full of blue and listened to harsh cawing just east. The air was still, the cornstalks motionless. To my right a small spider checked out his web between stiff leaves and settled down to wait for breakfast.

Slowly I sat up, hugged my knees and tried to remember if I'd ever slept on the ground sober before. I hadn't, and while it was nice not to have a headache, my body felt just as stiff as it always did when I woke from a bender.

Raising my head cautiously, I surveyed the bright world around me and squinted east where the red sun had just cleared a low hill.

The sun and walking worked out my stiffness and built an appetite which was close to dangerous by the time I reached town, but of course there wasn't anything open or anybody around except a milkman. I stopped by his wagon and bought a pint of white. The guy, figuring I was drunk, avoided my eyes and kept his distance to avoid any contamination. Even his horse looked disapproving.

At the first pay phone I dropped in a nickle and called the police station to report an attempted murder.

The cop was pretty thrilled about the idea that someone had been chasing me around in the night with a rifle. I could tell he was thrilled because he kept saying, "Oh, really?"

When he asked what time all of this happened and I said about two or so, he wanted to know why I was just reporting it.

"I just got back to town," I said.

"It took you all night to walk from Bender's Slough?"

"Well, I didn't come direct. I figured those jokers might hang around waiting for me to break cover so I waited in the cornfield till light."

"Uh-huh. And caught a little shut-eye meantime, eh?"

"Why, no. I was busy corn-holing a grasshopper. What the hell'd you think?"

"Don't get excited, pal. What's your name?"

I told him.

"Oh, yeah," he said. I recognized the tone.

"Look," I said, "you got anybody there that'd pick me up and maybe take me out to my car? I'd like to see if it's still there."

"Well, I'll tell you, Carl, our pick-up and delivery service takes Sundays off. Why don't you just hike on over here since you're already limbered up?"

"Will somebody take me out to my car if I do?"

"No, pal, I'm afraid not. We don't hardly ever go pull cars out of swamps when drunks run off the road on a Saturday night, no matter how great stories they tell. You think about it awhile and I bet you'll figure out why."

"Okay, but do yourself a favor, chief. Leave a note on Lieutenant Baker's desk. Tell him I called. Tell him somebody tried to bushwhack me. I'll be around to see him tomorrow."

"Sure, pal, I'll leave him your note and I know he'll just sure as hell be on tenterhooks till you show up with your whole story."

An hour later I'd talked a Standard station owner I knew into pumping a gallon of gas and loaning me a can and then I hitchhiked out to the car. Traffic was almost nothing, but in those days only the rich'd pass you up and none of them were out of bed yet. After my experience with the cop I didn't even think about telling the kid that picked me up how I happened to wind up in the ditch. I said I fell asleep.

The car was okay, hardly in up to the hubs in front, and with some help from the kid, about half a ton of gravel and a little pull with my chain, I was back on the road and on my way.

Church bells were ringing all over Corden by the time I reached town and I was pulling into the back lot when my old man, Elihu, came out, all duded up for church. His glare was enough to flatten a sensitive man. I could almost sympathize with him. The duds I wore were the same I'd slept in all night and they hadn't been improved much by the work involved in getting his car out of the swamp, and of course I needed a shave. But what really got to him was seeing his pet Dodge looking as spiffy as me.

I gave him a bright smile and said good morning. He snorted, moved past me, carefully avoiding contact, and walked around the Dodge.

"I might've known," he said in a strangled voice. "Trust you one minute with anything in the world and you muck it up—"

"There's nothing wrong with your pet that a wash job

won't cure. Not a scratch or dent—"

"It looks like old shit. And you had it all night—"

"Well, for god's sake, a car isn't like a virgin—what's all night got to do with it?"

"It's got everything to do with it. You weren't to go hounding around all night. I loaned it to you for a little trip and you've been God knows where—"

He was roaring by then and Bertha showed up, filling the back doorway like a fat cork and scowling at me.

"Well, damn!" I yelled. "For a man that was still yelling get a horse just five years ago, your love affair with that pile of tin is a howl—"

"Never you mind. You'll never get in that hunk of tin again I'll guarantee you that—"

It went on some more. Our fights always hit the high road early. I've never had hollering arguments with anybody else in my life and I've never argued with the old man in a civil tone yet. When I finally got enough sense to leave him and start inside, Bertha wouldn't budge until I cleaned mud off my shoes and then told me to get my muddy ass through her kitchen and not stop.

"Bertha," I said, "I haven't had a bite since yesterday noon."

The notion of anybody missing a meal, let alone two, shocked her so bad she stood with her mouth open long enough to catch flies before she recovered and told me to clean up and come back.

Half an hour later I was shaved, brushed, freshly clothed and sitting at the kitchen table sweet as a cherub. To pay for my orange juice, fried eggs, cinnamon toast and bacon with coffee, I had to listen to Bertha rant about how I was breaking old Elihu's heart and killing my mother. Since Elihu's heart was too small to break with anything but a jeweler's chisel and you couldn't kill Ma with an ax, I wasn't deeply moved. On the other hand, Bertha cooked so fine I was forced to break down and promise I'd reform, and then she told me if there was anything she couldn't stand it was a god-damned liar, I'd never change and why'd she bother to try and improve me. I promised to spend the rest of the day trying to figure that out for her.

The problem with the old man is, he never liked me because I had two older brothers and he'd always wanted a baby girl. When I was born with a penis he was so damned mad he didn't speak to Ma for a week. Then he decided to ignore facts and wouldn't let Ma cut my hair. At three years I had ringlets all around my ears and that's probably why I've been fighting all my life. Ma finally got disgusted and had my hair cut when I was four, and that time the old man didn't speak to her for a month. It didn't bother her any that I noticed. She was always willing to talk for two.

Anyway, the atmosphere around the hotel stayed sour all Sunday and I was relieved when Monday rolled around and I could take off for Aquatown—in my truck.

Chapter XIV

There was a different sergeant at the desk when I walked into the police station a little after nine A.M. The sign said his name was Wendworth, and I guessed as a kid he'd been called Windy, but that'd been a long time ago. He looked ripe for retirement with his deep wrinkles, big nose and tough double chin. His watery blue eyes wandered over my face, hands and clothes as I explained who I was and asked to see Lieutenant Baker.

"Carl Wilcox," he said thoughtfully. "You're the guy that ran his car into the slough Saturday night."

"I know."

"How old are you?"

"Thirty-four."

"I thought you'd be older."

"In February, will be."

"Uh-huh. You know, Carl, it seems like been hearing about you for forty years. How many times you been convicted?"

"Who counts?"

"Cops. Was it three?"

"Two."

"And you was married to a chorus girl from New York, right?"

"That wasn't a prison offense."

He grinned, showing tobacco-stained teeth.

"Did you really show up at a funeral riding a mule backwards?"

"Just at the cemetary. It wouldn't go into the church. How about you tell Baker I'm here?"

"I don't have to tell him. He's just sitting back there waiting for you. Don't pay any attention to the rubber hose on his desk. He only uses it for a fly-swatter."

Baker hollered "Yeah!" when I knocked on his door and looked up from a file on his desk as I walked in. I didn't see any rubber hose handy. Maybe he'd put it in the drawer over Sunday and hadn't got around to digging it out yet.

"You'd ought to close down on Sundays," I told him as I took the chair and moved it over to the wall again before sitting down.

"We will, as soon as people like you start going to church. Didn't you like our Sunday man?"

"He's a very cynical fellow. Needs church and faith."

"Probably. Tell me about Saturday night."

I did.

He watched me all the time, staring through his thick-lensed glasses that blurred his eyes so bad it seemed he had to be blind. Every so often he'd twitch his shoulders and shift in his chair as if he were impatient, anxious to get up and move or slug somebody, but his face was expressionless. When I was through he sat still a moment, then hunched his shoulders and rubbed his nose.

"You figure the men in the cornfield were the same you saw on the beach?"

"The guy with the rifle, the big one, could've been. If I caught the little one in the mouth during the beach scrap, don't think he'd have been feeling frisky enough. On the other hand he didn't have anything to do but drive and make with the flashlight. He might've been mad enough to ignore a broken tooth or so."

"But when he came at you on the rock, this big guy wasn't armed, right?"

"I don't know. I didn't frisk him."

"Uh-huh. Well, it could be they wanted to make it look like you got killed in an ordinary brawl. That wouldn't exactly surprise anybody around here. When it turned out too tough that way, they got sore and brought out the artilley. Which brings us to why'd they give a shit about you in the first place. Who've you talked to so far?"

"Sig French and his wife, the cousins; and Polly Erickson, a neighbor girl, guess you know her; and the Ryders—"

"Hugh Ryder?"

"I don't know his first name—he's got a cabin at the lake and his woman was friends with Kate."

"That's Hugh. Was there anybody else?"

"Doc Franklin and his daughter, Fancy."

We sat in silence for a while, and finally I asked how come he seemed to believe my story about Saturday night.

"I talked with Lou Corsi."

"You know Lou pretty well."

"He's my brother-in-law." The confessioon seemed to embarrass hm. Since it was obvious he had mostly accepted Lou's report on me I figured he liked Lou and still couldn't accept the idea that any in-law could be okay.

"I wasn't sure he'd really swallowed my story of the beach party."

"He did. He says you weren't drunk and claims you don't lie when you're sober hardly ever."

"How'd you happen to talk with him?"

"I had the word out that I wanted to know what you did."

I gaped. "You mean your guys are watching me?"

"Don't flatter yourself. That's not an army."

I snorted and got up.

"It'd be real smart," he said, "if you paddled back to Corden and kept your nose clean. I don't need any more dead bodies."

"Those guys on the beach wouldn't have been friends of yours, would they?" I asked.

He smiled, sweet as Little Red Riding Hood's wolf. "Who knows who his friends are these days?"

"Sure as hell cops don't," I said, and left him.

Chapter XV

I had a hamburger without onions at the Cozy Corner Café and drank a glass of milk for dinner, stopped by the pool hall and shot a round but couldn't sucker anyone into a paying game. Everybody in the place was either sober or knew me. There wasn't a poker game going either. So a little before dusk I thought about Avril, remembered Ryder's reverse invitation and made a telephone call to see if she might be alone. She was. I offered to take her for a ride. She thought about it and I asked was she scared of Ryder or just afraid of hurting his feelings and she said screw Ryder, come and get her.

She was wearing a green and white striped dress that didn't fit too well and made her look taller and skinnier than I remembered, but she'd just washed her hair so it was all soft and fluffy around her tanned face. At first she was in a bad mood. I suspected she was annoyed that I'd worked around her with the question about Ryder. I offered her a beer at the Wooden Palace and she said no thanks, we weren't getting together for romance, we were working on a murder. That made me wonder if she'd worn the green and white dress on purpose, knowing it didn't do anything for her, or did she just have bum taste?

I parked the truck in a lot near the Palace and we got out to stroll up toward the bluff overlooking the point. The wind had died down and the lake mirrored silver streaks from the setting sun. We walked along a path through parched grass and made our way uphill until we were on the bare knoll which was surrounded by woods, like thinning hair around a bald scalp.

Avril tilted her head toward the lake and said, "It looks so flat you'd think you could walk on it, wouldn't you?"

"Not in these shoes."

She looked at my feet and smiled, and in the soft light of the early evening she became a young and pretty girl.

"You have very small feet," she said, and then raised her eyes to my face and stopped. I came to a halt, facing her.

"You're not very tall. On the telephone you sound very different."

"A telephone makes me sound tall?"

"That's not really what I mean. It's, well, that first night I met you, and we were in the dark, all of my impressions came from your voice. I could hear it after you'd gone and I was in bed and from what I remembered I sort of built a man in my mind—"

"So it was a jolt when the real thing showed up in the daylight, huh?"

"Well, don't be annoyed, you weren't what I expected. First impressions always stick with me and since then, when I see you, it mixes me up."

"Maybe we could fix you up with a blindfold."

"No, I'll adjust. How tall *are* you?"

"Does that really make a hell of a lot of difference?"

"No, I just—"

"Like you said, we're not getting together for romance, we're working on a murder."

She dropped her eyes and sighed. "I guess you're more sensitive than you look. I'd have guessed that from the voice, but head on you're so self-assured and kind of cocky."

"Well, in the dark I saw you different too."

She lifted her head and grinned. "Shorter and rounder, I bet."

"And older."

"Older? Why?"

"The low voice."

"How old do you think I am?"

"How dumb do you think I am? I'm not gonna answer a question like that."

She laughed, took my arm and we started walking up the hill again.

"The most I know about you," she said, "is that Ryder's told me lots of stories. You've been in lots of trouble, fight a lot, have all kinds of girls. He's very jealous and envious so I assume he's exaggerating, but what do you really do? Wnat would you do if you could have anything you wanted?"

"What I do right now is drive a truck when I can get a job, which is damned seldom, and help hold a falling-down hotel together when I have to, which is often. If I had my rathers I'd be a beachcomber in the South Pacific with a private still, a good sailboat and a cast-iron gut. But right now I'd like to know a way to get Boswell out of jail."

"Would he like beachcombing?"

"He likes Corden and his shack by the railroad. And

he'd like some grandchildren. He'll never have any because he never had a wife or kids."

"I guess you've never had any kids, either."

"No."

"Don't you like them?"

"Sure. I like cats and dogs, too, but I've never had
any since I was little."

"You had a dog then?"

"No, it was a cat, named Gans, after the fighter. He
was damned near big as a dog, and smart. He could
open a latch-string door. Just reared up and pulled the
latch. Used to jump on my shoulder. So damned big he
nearly flattened me the first time he pulled that."

She'd had a collie. A big, beautiful bitch. "Only she
was terribly stupid. They breed them with such narrow
skulls they don't have room for brains, you know."

When we came to where the hill sloped off sharply toward the beach about seventy feet below, Avril sat
down in the long grass. I sat close beside her.

"I guess maybe we should talk about Kate," she said
in a withdrawing tone.

I said fine, pulled out my tobacco bag and began
rolling a cigaret. "Want one?" I asked. She shook her
head. It seemed like she had something on her mind
she wanted to unload but was holding back. I couldn't
decide whether I should try to prime the pump or just
keep my mouth shut and wait until she was ready to
spring it her own way.

"You know something?" she said suddenly. "Ryder's very worried about you."

"He got something to worry about?"

"He thinks so. He's jealous. I'm not supposed to
talk with you alone or let you into the cabin. He says you
have a really terrible reputation with the ladies."

When I met her eyes she smiled and turned to look at the darkening lake.

"Do you two fight a lot?" I asked.

"Not a lot."

"He ever hit you?"

"You think I'd stick around if he did?"

"I guess not."

"I'd flatten him with a frying pan."

"What'd you say when he told you I had this awful reputation?"

"I told him mine wasn't too great either."

"That must've been a great pacifier."

She shrugged. "I'm not a pacifying woman."

"I thought maybe you told him he didn't have to worry since I wasn't tall."

She turned her head my way and frowned. "That really worries you, doesn't it?"

"Not that much."

"You want a woman you can look down on."

"No, all I can't abide is one too fat to get my arm around."

"You don't mind them slim?"

"I love 'em slim."

"Actually I'm closer to skinny than slim. Ryder takes my being skinny as a criticism of his fat. He says if I'd put on some weight I'd be more tolerant and good-natured."

"I thought you two didn't talk about personal things."

"Like being skinny or fat? Well, I don't say anything about *him* being a lard-ass, but we do talk about each other now and again. What we don't talk about is going to bed—or not going to bed, which is the case."

She apparently thought about bed a lot. That was

fine, I thought about it a lot too. I was thinking about it now and wondered why, because I did think she was too bony for my taste, but I liked the way her hair fluffed around her face and the colt awkwardness of her long legs and the half-tough attitudes. Of course mostly I liked it that she was interested and curious. The worst thing old Ryder could've done for his case was to tell her I was hell with the ladies. That was really stupid. He couldn't have helped me more.

She leaned a little toward me and said, "I'll bet you're thinking about Kate."

"Kate who?"

She grinned and there was enough light left to show her white teeth. "Don't kid me, you've got a one-track mind. She's all you ever really want to talk about."

"Well, isn't that why we get together?"

"I'm not so sure. The way Ryder talks, I thought maybe I was being hustled."

"And you're still willing to come along?"

"It looks that way, doesn't it? Maybe I like the way you roll a cigaret. Is it true you were married to a chorus girl?"

"No. She was a vaudeville musician."

"Oh? What'd she play?"

"A banjo."

"A *banjo*?" She started to laugh. "I never heard of a woman banjo player."

"She was the best-looking one in New York."

"Probably the only one."

"She was the only one I ever saw," I admitted.

That tickled her so it took a while before she managed to ask what'd happened to the lady.

"Damned if I know. She's probably banjoing someplace back east."

"But you were married?"

"Uh-huh."

"And you brought her back to the hotel?"

"Yup, right after Armistice."

"You wanted your parents to see her, right?"

"Couldn't wait."

"What happened?"

"Well, I hadn't told Mitzi much more than enough to let her imagination go. And like most liars, she had more imagination than hell's got boarders, so she pictured the Wilcox Hotel as maybe one notch below the Grand. When she saw the real thing she changed colors three times and told me she'd seen bigger outhouses. When Ma saw Mitzi, *she* changed colors four times before she managed to work up a hello smile. My old man, Elihu, he just stood and stared with his jaw dropped about to his belly button."

"I heard you liked practical jokes, but that one sounds too far-fetched."

"It was. I quit after that. Didn't know any way to top it."

"Wasn't it awfully cruel?"

"Not if you knew Mitzi, or Ma. People like that, you can't really faze 'em or teach 'em. They got the whole world figured out and nothing's going to happen that stops them for longer than to make some profound remark like, 'Well, that's just like a man!' "

She hugged her knees and rocked back and forth, giggling.

"I guess you thought they had a lot in common, huh?"

"All I know is, when Mitzi got the divorce, Ma was sadder than when the transplanted elm died. She told me Mitzi may have dressed like a floozie, but she had a good heart. Somehow she never noticed that till after Mitzi left."

"Were you sad when she left?"

"I was more like damned relieved. For a while there I was scared to death Mitzi'd decide to become the belle of Corden and stick around. She got so much attention I could've put her on show and sold tickets. Everybody in Corden County came around for a look."

"How'd you meet her?"

"On an elevator. I think it was going down. Now how about we talk about Ryder and you?"

"I'd rather not."

"Well, that's how I feel about Mitzi and me. So we're back to Kate. You think she learned something new lately that got her started on digging up ancient history?"

She quit hugging her knees, propped her hands behind her and looked up at the sky.

"I guess, right at this minute, I don't want to talk about Kate. For a little while there, I actually forgot the awful thing that's happened and what I've been doing with myself lately, and I was having fun. I want to know some more about you. You're a very strange and unusual guy. Nothing about you makes sense and I guess I think nothing about me does either and we should have a lot in common."

"You like practical jokes?"

"No, I've just lived one."

I leaned toward her. "How about I go get us something to drink and we have a real talk?"

"Don't try to get me drunk. That kind of business makes me sick."

"What I've got wouldn't get *one* drunk, let alone two, but it'd be enough to make a small party."

"I don't know. . . ."

"You wait here, I'll be right back."

I moved fast back to the truck, dug out my pint, took the blanket from behind the seat and ran back up the hill. It seemed a little risky, taking the blanket. She might be spooked and blow the whole ball, but being shy's never got me anything so I took the chance.

At sight of the blanket she sat up straight.

"What've you got in mind?" she demanded.

"Keeping our bottoms off the ground, okay?"

"I'm not going to lie down."

"Okay, don't panic."

To calm her I folded the blanket so it was just big enough to let us both sit comfortably and passed her the bottle.

"Is this some of Boswell's moon?" she asked, taking a sniff.

"Yup. Guaranteed quality, gentler than lightning and smooth as wax."

She tilted the bottle and sipped.

"It's not bad," she allowed. "Tastes easier than what Ryder buys."

"Who does he buy from?"

She said she didn't know. After we'd both sampled the moon a couple times I stuck the cork back in and put the bottle by my side. We talked, not saying much and I kissed her. I did it gentle, without hands, and moved away before she did. The next time I got an arm around her and pretty soon her hands were on the back of my head, pressing ever so easy. Finally she lowered her head and slowly pushed me away.

"I think maybe you *are* dangerous," she said. "You

must have shaved early this morning, your whiskers are like wire."

"If I'd had any notion of how things were going to go, I'd have brought a razor."

She laughed. "Kate used to say the only thing a man's face was good for was as a back-scratcher."

"You got an itch?"

She wouldn't admit it. Like most women, she wanted lots of slow buildup. I suppose that comes from the fact that most guys, once they get down to business, have a sex attention span shorter than their tools and if a girl's going to have any fun she'd got to get it during preliminaries.

"I suppose you think I'm a loose woman," she said as we settled down side by side.

"You're just independent," I assured her. "How about we spread this blanket out so you won't get grass stains?"

"All right, but let's move over under the trees. I don't like being in the middle of a clearing."

She was a little stiff when we got settled the second time. I hoped she wouldn't ask if I'd respect her afterward.

"I just absolutely won't belong to anyone," she told me, "like a pet dog or a slave. I've seen too much of that. I'll do as I please."

"Good for you. Is that how Kate felt?"

That was a mistake. She popped up on one elbow and glared down at me. "I didn't get my independence from her. We were friends because we thought alike from the start."

"But she didn't like men."

"She did so. Why else would she encourage so many and have been married?"

"I've known guys who kept dogs that didn't mean anything to them but something they could kick around and cuss."

She considered that about a second, laughed, and settled down again.

"It wasn't really that bad with Kate. There were times I had a feeling that men scared her and that she kept them around to prove to herself she wasn't a coward. She was the sort of person who has to face fear down. Like, if she got that panicky urge to run out of a dark basement, she'd deliberately turn around and walk back into it."

Kate was beginning to bore me. Mostly I was thinking about how I could get Avril worked up for action, but as I shifted around to try kissing her again I sighted two figures strolling over the rise about a dozen yards east of us. One was taller and their silhouettes blurred against the trees so I couldn't tell whether they were lovers or the two spooks who'd been haunting me.

"What's the matter?" whispered Avril, twisting to see what I was staring at.

"Stay down!"

She was suspicious, but after a glance at the approaching pair she went flat. The walkers came on slowly, then turned toward the point and stopped, facing the lake. The tall one put an arm around the smaller one.

"It's all right," I whispered.

"Did you think we'd been followed?"

"I thought maybe."

After a short, frightened silence she asked, "Have you been followed before?"

"Uh-huh." I kept my eyes on the couple. Either they were married or he was a damned slow mover.

"Do you know who's been doing it?"

"No."

Carefully she lifted her head and rose on one elbow. "What're they doing?"

"Sitting down. It's okay. Just a guy and his girl."

She got to her knees and stared toward the couple who had moved past the hillcrest and were out of sight.

"Let's go spy on them."

I looked at her and she laughed softly. "Didn't you ever do that when you were a kid? Sneak up and watch couples that didn't know you were there?"

"No." I didn't admit I'd harrassed a few.

"Well, it's time you did, come on!"

Since we weren't getting anywhere on our blanket, I shrugged and went along as she crept up the slope toward the point. From what I'd seen I didn't figure this pair meant business so I was pretty surprised when, as we topped the rise, we looked down and saw white skin glowing in the dark. There was no moon but the stars were working all out and this guy was working all in. His partner's legs were up so far her knees rubbed his armpits and his skinny bottom was bouncing like a dribbled basketball. However slow he was at getting started, once in action he could beat a rabbit. Avril gasped, clutched my arm and crouched down, watching in fascination. We could hear sounds, low and rapid, a grunt at each stroke, in unison. Soon the guy lost steam, faltered and stopped. The raised legs locked across his back in a spasm and he fell on her, quivering.

"Weak wind-up," I whispered.

Avril jabbed me with her elbow and kept watching. The couple didn't stir.

"I think she snapped his spine," I whispered.

Avril smothered a laugh, turned away and pulled me with her. We moved in a shuffling crouch back to the

blanket and before even stretching out we were kissing
open-mouthed and fumbling with clothes.

"Don't hurry!" she panted and I promised I wouldn't
while grabbing everything choice as fast as it was un-
covered and nothing seemed bony at all. It was all frantic, mostly awkward and lovely as hell. She raised too
high when I was ready to start and said, "No, not
there," and we both laughed, and then she cuffed me
one and quick as a terrier, rolled on top. Since I'm used
to having my rear in the air during such parties I felt
tied up—as if I were being forced to fight a match
lefthanded—but she was so happy and great I decided
what the hell, see how the other half lives. The trouble
with that was I lost control and shot early. She never
knew the difference and kept moving with such enthusiasm I figured it could be fatal if I quit so I stayed with
her. When she finally got over the rise she started a
whoop that I corked with a hand slapped over her
mouth. The next moment she was dead asleep. I mean,
she changed from a combination wildcat and bucking
bronc to a sleeping kitten as if I'd been pumping her
full of knockout drops.

When I eased her shoulders over to one side so I
could look around, she gripped me tight for a second
and went limp again.

Later I slipped out from under, covered her carefully
with the blanket and pulled on my pants. In a bed with
the door locked and some reasonable notion that I'm
not going to be stumbled over by strangers, I'm more
than willing to dream and doze and even think about another round, but God knows there's nothing more vulnerable in the world than a man with his pants down
and his ass bare to the world.

I sat beside her for quite a while, listening to leaves rustle in the wind and hearing occasional snatches of music from the Wooden Palace. Finally I got up and pussyfooted over to look at the other lovers.

They were gone.

For a second I wondered if they'd come over to see our show, but I decided they were too self-centered to notice. I went back to Avril, put my hand on her bare shoulder and stirred her gently.

"Mmmf?"

"Better get dressed."

She stirred, raised her head, pushed her short hair back and smiled at me.

"Is breakfast ready?"

"Not quite."

"Good, let's do it again."

"I'd be afraid. You pass out too cold afterward. I thought you were dead."

"Can't you do it again?"

"Not here."

"Where?"

"I don't know. . . ."

"How about in your truck?"

"That's a hell of a place for loving—"

She sat up and patted my hand kindly. "It's all right if you can't."

She dressed while I folded up the blanket and took my hand as we walked back toward my truck.

About fifteen minutes later I turned off the highway, took a county road for a mile and a half and made another turn under a wrought-iron arch. As we drove down the narrow dirt road Avril suddenly clutched my arm.

"Hey! This is a cemetery."

"Right. And it's on top of a hill so we can see any-body coming, it's got enough trees to keep us hidden, and none of the neighbors are gonna complain or gossip. And if you really conk out this time, think of how handy."

She started laughing and held my arm with both hands.

"Oh, God, what a nut!"

She was doubtful about straddling me in the seat at first but once under way worked up an easy rhythm so perfect I thought we might just keep it up through next week. Then I started thinking maybe she worked so well from on top because that's the way she'd been doing it with Ryder since he got so fat. Before that no-tion could make me limp, she started giving me the squeezy touch and whispered in my ear so nice I forgot about him and everything was so lovely it seemed a time to die.

After conking out the second time, Avril was too far gone to even murmur as I lifted her off and parked her beside me. She didn't stir a few minutes later when I opened the door, slipped clear and left her sleeping across the seat.

Leaning against the truck side I felt warm inside, cool on my skin and content as a freshly nursed kitten. It seemed still enough to hear corn growing in the near field (my old man swears you can hear it on July nights), but unless the sound is the same as crickets fiddling, I didn't catch it.

Avril woke when I climbed back in the cab and gen-tly lifted her shoulders from the seat. After a couple kisses she sat erect and touched her whisker-rubbed face.

"I'm going to tell you something now. Maybe I should have before, maybe I shouldn't now, but I'm going to . . ."

"I'm gonna have to shave closer?" I suggested as I moved my foot toward the starter.

"No, that'd be nice, but that's not it."

"It's pretty late. I'd better get you back—"

"You want to know about Kate?"

"Well, sure—"

"What happened to her fingers was no accident. They were cut off by a kidnapper who sent her fingers to her parents, one at a time, to make her father pay ransom."

All of a sudden I was no longer sleepy.

"Tell me about it."

Chapter XVI

"It's such a wild story, Kate didn't think anybody'd believe it and she only told me when I swore on my soul I'd never breathe a word of it."

Avril rubbed her eyes, twisted in the seat and brought her left leg up so her knee was touching my thigh as she faced me.

"It happened when Kate was eight years old. She was taking her regular afternoon nap on a sun porch at the back of the house. She wasn't really asleep; she was too old for naps, but her mother insisted, probably to get her out of the way for a bit, so Kate'd lie there, daydreaming or playing with her cat, except when her mother came by and then she'd close her eyes and pretend. Only this time when someone came, Kate was gagged, blindfolded, tied and carried to a car. She told me she wasn't panicky, like you'd expect, and while she never admitted it, I think she guessed who was doing it from the start. Anyway, she said the car drove fast for a long ways. It seemed like hours and hours, and finally they stopped and she was carried inside and put in a little room with no windows, a canvas cot and a commode. It smelled moldy and was hot.

"There were two people. The one who talked was obviously a man. She guessed, from the sound of heels, the other was a woman. The man always whispered. He untied her, took off the gag and said she'd only be there a little while and she needn't worry. Everything'd be fine if she did as she was told and behaved like a good girl. She had to promise that every time he knocked on her door, she'd put on a little hood he had for her. If she ever failed or tried to cheat, she'd be kept blindfolded and tied up all the time. He told her she was beautiful and very brave and he knew she'd also be patient. And, as Kate told me, he was clever enough to know that she wanted approval more than anything, so of course she did exactly as he asked.

"They fed her three times a day—oatmeal for breakfast, a sandwich at noon and hamburgers at night. The first day was the longest of her life; there was nothing to do—she counted the floorboards, measured the room with her feet, tried to remember names of all the kids in her school. You remember how, when you were a kid, time dragged? She became so absolutely bored that when the man knocked on her door she wanted to hug him the moment he came in. She told him how bored she was and begged for crayons and a drawing book or something to read or play with. In the morning he brought her some chalk and said she could mark the floor and play tic-tac-toe or hopscotch and he left a pack of cards. They were old and greasy, but she made the best use of them—they were dolls, toy soldiers and building material.

"When he came in the third day he was very upset. He said her daddy wasn't being cooperative and if he didn't change she couldn't go home and something terrible would happen. He didn't joke or give her compliments, and for the first time she was afraid. He sensed her fear, she told me, and said it wasn't his fault, it was all her daddy's. All he had to do was give them a little of the big amount he had which they desperately needed and then Kate could go back home, but no, he was stingy and mean and didn't love her. She wasn't inclined to doubt him. Timmerman wasn't exactly a doting father. He wasn't mean—never struck her or yelled. Mostly he was distant and indifferent, and that was tough on Kate because she was naturally affectionate. Her mother was a little strange—she'd be over-affectionate one time and cold as January the next and Kate was sure she didn't care a damn for Timmerman. Both mother and daughter were happiest when he was at work or, better yet, on a trip out of town.

"On the fourth day the whispering man came in and the woman was with him. She was silent, as always, but the man spoke to her a few times. He whispered to Kate—she said it now had a hissing sound—and said Timmerman had to be taught a lesson. When the man took her hand and spread her fingers on the floor, she was still trusting, but her first panic came from the cruel firmness of the grip on her wrist just before the lightning stab of pain that shot up her arm, through her shoulder and clear to her brain. The crash of the ax and her own scream were all one part of the agony and shock . . ."

Avril's voice stuck in her throat and she turned her head to stare out through the windshield a moment. After swallowing hard several times, she went on.

"The woman joined the man in making her unclasp the hand and let them wrap the wound, and the man cried and swore as he held her in his lap and hugged her close, saying it was all Timmerman's fault. He'd never wanted to hurt her and he'd not do it again if

Timmerman would only pay the money and save them all.

"They gave her sleeping pills and the woman stayed in the room until Kate slept. The next day they cleaned and put a fresh bandage on the wound.

"They cut off the second finger on the seventh day. It was much worse than the first time and Kate couldn't talk about it at all. She cried when she remembered it. They wrapped the severed fingers up, one at a time, and mailed them by first class. Kate never heard what happened when those packages arrived, no one in the family could ever speak of it. I suspect Timmerman knew who was behind it. At least Kate felt sure of that. Kate's mother told her over and over that it took a long time to get the money because the amount was so high her father had trouble making arrangements. Kate thought Timmerman embezzled the ransom money from his own bank rather than touch his savings and investments and that was why it took so long, but she admitted she had no proof. She even admitted it wasn't likely he'd have as much as they demanded, but somehow she had to make Timmerman the villain because she just couldn't put all the blame on the kidnappers. I never could understand that. To me that man was the most despicable beast imaginable—a man who'd mutilate a trusting child for money, and then slobber over her and blame her father for what he'd done to her. Jesus, that makes me boil!

"Kate never heard how the payment was handled. The whole thing was just never talked about, but when the money was delivered they drove Kate to a road south of the Cities and let her out and telephoned the Timmermans to say where she was. The Timmermans had been staying in a Minneapolis Hotel and they drove to the address and found Kate. She remembered hearing a lot of argument between her parents about when she'd be taken to a doctor. Ellie, Kate's mother, wanted to take her directly to a hospital, but he wouldn't have that. They'd take her to his doctor in Aquatown. He didn't want the police to know anything. He claimed it was because the kidnappers had threatened to kill Kate if the police were told. So they drove Kate all the way home, sitting on her mother's lap and her mother cried all the way."

I tossed my cigaret out the open truck window to the dusty road and patted the knee that Avril had pressed against my right thigh.

"Why'd Kate think her old man knew who kidnapped her?"

"I'm not certain. Kate *said* it was because the whispering man seemed to know Timmerman so well. He talked to Kate about him as if she and he had an understanding between them and old Timmerman was outside it all. The man told her that having to pay to get back would make Timmerman appreciate her because he only appreciated things that cost him cash. He said Kate was a gift to her father from her mother and hadn't cost him enough. He used that phrase, 'the gift of Kate,' as if it were a line from a poem. Isn't that weird?"

"Was all this before the hatchet work?"

"Before *and* after. He talked with her afterward in the same conspiratorial way. After the second cutting he promised he'd never hurt her again. She didn't believe him, but she still didn't completely hate him. Fear became almost everything, but she said animal cunning made her know if she weren't hateful he'd be less likely to hurt her. At the time she thought she'd managed to make him care about her. Later she thought he was only taking advantage to make her easier to handle. I'm not so sure myself. If that was all there was to it, why'd he cry when he let her out of the car and why'd he kiss her mutilated hand and say he was sorry?"

"Maybe it was something like the hunters getting sentimental of their kills. The this-hurts-me-more-than-it-does-you bullshit that parents tell kids before they whale them."

That didn't satisfy her any more than it did me, and for a while we sat quietly. Then she took my hand and leaned against my shoulder.

"What doctor'd they take Kate to in Aquatown?" I asked.

"Old Jay Lewis. He died ten years ago."

"Did he have a regular nurse?"

"There was a woman who worked for him, I don't think she was a registered nurse. She moved away a long time ago."

"Did anybody ever ask where this camp was that Kate was supposed to have gone to?"

"I don't think so. People just accept things told them by Timmerman types. He was awfully intimidating."

"Let's talk about Kate's trips to Minneapolis."

"Well, like I told you, I thought she maybe had found someone there. And she liked to buy clothes in their stores and go to plays and concerts. She said she felt it was necessary for people from South Dakota to make some kind of obeisance to civilization. Now, as I keep thinking about her last trips, I think maybe she was seeing someone who was looking into the kidnapping business. She mentioned a strange name once—something like Julius Giles."

"What brought that on?"

"Well, I'd told her once I was thinking of leaving Ryder, and she said it was too bad I wasn't married to him because she knew a guy who'd been a divorce lawyer and he'd be ideal to break us up. I asked how come she knew him and she said it was from when she'd been married and was thinking of a divorce for herself, before her husband drowned. Look, lover-boy, I'm too sleepy for more talk. Take me home."

Ryder's car was parked beside the back door when we arrived, and I asked Avril if she expected he'd give her any trouble for coming in so late.

"Don't be silly," she said as she got out.

"Maybe I'd better stick around a while."

"That'd be the worst possible thing. Just scoot. And call me tomorrow, okay?"

I watched her to the door. There were no lights inside. She turned at the stoop, threw me a kiss and then made a shooing motion with both hands. I drove off, feeling very uneasy.

Chapter XVII

I woke in the morning feeling smug and wishing all I had to worry about was getting another party with Avril. Then I thought about her bear friend, Ryder. It seemed likely she was right about him not turning on her, but on the other hand, jealousy's like a tornado—you never know what direction it'll take or where it'll hit ground.

Bertha fed me breakfast in the kitchen and I was enjoying the scrambled eggs and bacon until Elihu showed up. He handed me his usual line about was I up for all day and then launched into suggestions for the order of business. First make a trash haul to the dump, then hoe vegetables in the garden up on the hill, replace a mess of rotting boards on the balcony . . . .

"How about I shove a broom stick up my ass and sweep while I'm running around?" I asked.

"Fine."

"What're you gonna pay me for all these chores?"

"Same I been paying that you haven't earned in the past thirty years—room and board."

"The board's almost worth it," I allowed, "but I got a problem that calls for cash."

"Don't try robbing for it. You ain't got the knack."

"Yeah, I know, you already told me. What do you think of old Boswell?"

"I think he's just about what you're gonna be thirty years from now—an old bum."

"You think he'd ought to hang?"

He snorted. "He won't hang. Not even that idiot in Aquatown's dumb enough to think Boswell'd kill anybody. He's just got to hold him until he finds another goat. If you're smart, you'll stay out of the way and not get picked to take his place."

"Oh, no. This is one time I'm not the patsy. Joey's talked to Baker, so's Lou Corsi. They got Baker sold on me. But I need money for a trip to Minneapolis. There's a guy there—"

Elihu shook his white head. "Huh-uh. The last time you went to the Cities you got drunk and stuck up a jewelry store. I ain't paying for another toot like that. Get your money from Baker if he's so sold on you."

"I figured you'd be understanding."

He finally agreed to pay for one tank of gas if I did his chores, so I went at it. Late in the afternoon I was halfway through the balcony repair job when Elihu came up to tell me there was a phone call for me.

A moment later I was talking with Sig French.

"Lorna and I've been talking," he said in his cheerful voice, "and we've decided to go back home, but we don't want to leave things just hanging, so to speak, and I wondered if you still wanted to help your friend."

"I never stop wanting to help friends."

He laughed. "That's what I figured. Well, let me ask you—what'd you charge to make a little investigation for us? It hadn't ought to be much since you're already doing it free."

"You offering to hire me as a private eye?"

"Uh, something like that. What'd you charge? I can't afford anything big, of course, but I want to see the effort made and I hear you've already solved a couple cases, right? And I don't think much of this Lieutenant Baker, to tell you the truth. I talked to him a lot and he doesn't impress me."

I wondered how much of the talk had been about me.

"What'll you pay?" I asked.

"Well," I could picture him squirming, "what'll you need?"

"Ten dollars a day and expenses."

"I'll give you five, but I don't pay for meals—"

"Come on, French, don't try to chisel a small-town boy. I'm no good at this Gypsy stuff."

"Okay, I'll teach you how it goes: Now you say how about eight a day and then I offer seven and we compromise on seven-fifty."

"How about ten?"

"You want to help your buddy out?"

"Will you back me for a trip to Minneapolis?"

There was a moment of silence. Then he asked, "Why do you want to go to Minneapolis?"

"Kate's friend, Avril, gave me the name of a guy Kate was seeing on her last trips there."

"Really? Who was that?"

"Fella named Julius Giles. Ever heard of him?"

He started to laugh. After a second he said she had to have made up that name. I said it was the only lead I had.

"Okay," he said at last. "I'll stake you to the trip, but I'm putting a two-week limit on this ten-dollar-a-day business, and you can't spend it all in Minneapolis."

"You want to go through the motions or do you want to nail Kate's killer?"

"I'm anxious to do my duty but I'm not ready to go bust. Do what you can. If you make progress we'll talk again in two weeks."

"You going to write up a contract?"

"No, this is just between you and me."

"Okay, I need an advance for expenses."

He finally agreed to $100. I wished after I'd hung up that I'd demanded twelve a day and two hundred but having settled things I didn't stew about it.

When I parked behind Kate's place, Polly popped out of the cabin next door and intercepted me. Apparently she'd decided she had grown up. She was wearing shoes. She asked me what was happening. I told her I'd gone professional, Sig was paying me to make an investigation.

She glanced at Kate's cabin and peered into my eyes.

"Don't trust him."

"Why not? Because he lied about Kate writing?"

"That . . . and he's too friendly. There's something *wrong* about him."

"Gee, Polly, I'm a friendly guy too—"

She shook her head irritably, but before we could talk any more Sig stepped out on the back stoop and called, so I gave Polly a salute and went to join him.

"Polly's a cute kid, isn't she?" he said. "I love young girls—very properly, you understand—and they like me. Always been that way. Well, come on in."

The living room was a surprise. The couches, which had bracketed the fireplace, were now pushed back to the walls, making the room large and formal. The chair where Kate had died was gone from sight. Lorna sat in the couch by the windows overlooking the lake and was busy knitting. She looked younger in a pale blue dress, even though the tightly drawn-back hair gave her the look of a white-faced crow. I watched her brown and freckled hands working the knitting needles as if they had eyes of their own. She saw me looking around and pursed her lips.

"Kate's chair is in the spare room. I moved the couches to get rid of the clutter." She sounded defensive.

"Why not?"

"Sig thinks it wasn't respectful. As if Kate might come back and object. I think that's nonsense."

I glanced at Sig who looked at the ceiling and twisted his mouth clownishly.

"We're going to sell the place, so I felt we should make it look as roomy and pleasant as possible. There'll be trouble enough finding a buyer after what happened here."

I nodded, thinking how selfish it had been of Kate to get herself murdered and leave all these worries for Lorna. Outside the calm lake gleamed silver in the dying light.

Sig asked me to sit down, offered a drink, which I turned down, and then Lorna offered coffee and got up to get it when I agreed.

"Are you the only surviving relatives?" I asked Sig.

"Oh, yeah, sure."

"Did Kate leave a will?"

"Uh-huh. Her lawyer's got it."

"And she left you the place?"

"Well, there hasn't been a reading yet," he grinned a little sheepishly. "We haven't pushed anything . . . you know . . ."

"But you're planning to sell the place."

"Well, it doesn't hurt to start planning some . . . ."

Lorna returned with a tray of cups and saucers, a sugar bowl and cream pitcher and told Sig to go after the coffeepot, which he did. Then she bustled about, pouring and getting us organized. Sig watched her with a half-worried smile, and I had a sudden notion that perhaps she suffered from some secret, slow-killing disease which enslaved him through pity.

When we were into the coffee, Lorna took up her knitting once more and nailed me with a look like a crow eyeing a corncob.

"How do you solve a crime, Mr. Wilcox? I understand you've been involved in things like this before. What's your method?"

"I don't know that it's a method at all, Mrs. French. I just use a natural snoopy persistence."

"Well, how do you start?"

"By talking to people."

"Who? How do you decide?"

"I just pick anybody handy, and one thing leads to another—when I'm lucky."

"It sounds very haphazard. What's your lead now?"

"Well, I'm going on a little trip to Minneapolis."

The knitting movements skipped a beat as she looked up at me. "Minneapolis. That's hardly handy, is it?"

"You asked how I started. I didn't say I never went out of my way later on."

"And you've actually solved cases?"

"A few people think so."

It was obvious she wasn't among that few. She stabbed at her knitting for a while and I figured she wished it were me. No doubt she and old Sig had gone around and around before he convinced her that renting a hobo as a private eye could be anything but a wild waste of money. Hell, he hadn't convinced her of anything; he'd just got his way and she resented it.

I looked at Sig. "Seems to me you said something about an advance."

He gave a start as if he'd been goosed, turned red and said, "Yeah, sure," and went off toward the bedroom. When I stared after him, Lorna spoke.

"He's going after his checkbook. And, yes, I know he agreed to pay you to investigate. The notion's ludicrous, but it's typical of Sigfried to hire a nobody to hunt the murderer of a cousin he hasn't given a thought to for years but now assumes as his responsibility. It's the Don Quixotish part of him that makes him a clown, but he's a good man and he can't help it if he's never grown up."

She sounded like the women of the Wilcox clan convinced that every man is an overgrown boy. It's always galled me that my life has generally done nothing but confirm this dumb idea.

Sig came out of the bedroom, dangling a check between his thumb and forefinger, as if it were brittle and might crack.

"There you are," he said, shoving it my way.

I took it, examined the amount and signature and stuck it in my shirt pocket.

"Is it true you've sworn off drink?" demanded Lorna. It was an important question, I could tell, because she set her knitting aside and gave me a beady stare.

"Did Sig tell you that?"

She didn't look at him, and slowly nodded.

"You think he'd lie?"

She smiled and suddenly I could see a child behind the crow face. "No, but now and then he prevaricates, for my benefit."

"Well," I said, melted some by the discovery that she might actually have a sense of humor, "I don't take oaths, but don't worry—I won't go on a bender with your money."

She nodded, unconvinced, and picked up her knitting.

"How're you going to travel?" asked Sig, trying to bring a businesslike tone to the proceedings.

"Train."

"Passenger or freight?"

"Passenger. I've got a time limit, remember?"

"Two weeks, that's right."

"Depending on progress, you said."

He admitted that.

"So I go paid fare."

"Okay. I'm not a cheap man."

When I was about to leave he clasped my hand and gripped my arm in the old Rotary double sincere hold. I expected to see moisture in his blue eyes and it actually was there. It was as if he never expected to see me again. Sig was a genuine sentimentalist; he'd weep over a farewell with his own hangman.

"Keep in touch," he said huskily.

I promised I would.

Chapter XVIII

Wednesday night my train huffed into the Great Northern Depot at Minneapolis. A few minutes later I was hiking along with my ditty bag, being jostled by a few million Swedes loaded with baggage and anxiety, all in a tear to climb the stairs and see the big city. At the top we all popped into the giant waiting room with its ceiling half a mile high and walls covered with murky murals about Indians and plains and noble settlers. It bustled with folks buying tickets, spilling over the rows of wooden benches and charging to and from exits. I kept rubbernecking around, like a kid at his first circus.

Outside, on Hennepin Avenue, cabs were lined up and streetcars clattered by on their iron rails with their trolleys sparking along the overhead wires, and lights inside showed people packed in and staring out the open windows at the Fords, Chevvies, Packards, Cadillacs, Hudsons, Graham Paiges and God-knows-what-all. In Corden we almost never saw anything but black Model T's and green Chevvies; here they had everything.

I walked west along Hennepin, still gawking around as I approached the brighter lights. A panhandler, taking me for a hick, tried to bum a dime, but I told him I was working this side of the street and he snarled and moved on.

Since the dining car fare on the train had been too steep for my taste, I started looking for a café before worrying about a place to flop. The first joints along the avenue had menus chalked on blackboards out front and didn't look too appetizing so I moved on to where things got a little cleaner and tried a counter place that smelled something like the hamburger stands churches sponsor in the Corden Park during Fourth of July celebrations. For fifteen cents I got a fair hamburger with onions, ketchup and coffee. There was no pickle, but I got by.

Feeling full and flush I decided to hell with a flophouse and moved on to a one-flight-up hotel where I bought a private room with access to a toilet down the hall. It was a little scroungy and didn't smell as sweet as the Wilcox Hotel, but at least nobody'd be on me to do chores in the morning.

Leaving my bag in the room I went down to the public telephone and thumbed through a worn directory. There was more than one Giles but none with a Julius or a J. I tried Gyles and found it.

The wall clock behind the registration desk said nine-thirty-three as the operator put through my call. Four rings brought a husky voice that growled "Hello!" like an accusation.

"I understand you know Kate Bonney," I said.

"Who's this?"

I told him.

"Where you calling from?"

I told him that too.

"So what're you after?"

"Information. I want to know who killed her."

He wasn't surprised. "Why ask me?"

"You knew her, you'd been seeing her lately—"

"I can't help you." It didn't seem to break his heart.

"Look, it's damned important. An old guy's been accused of doing the job—"

"How old?"

"Over seventy."

"So he won't be in the can long."

"I just want to come around and talk with you. It might be worth your while, you know?"

"My while is worth money, friend. You handing out any?"

"It depends on what you know, if anything," I lied.

"Uh-huh."

He didn't believe me, but I got a feeling he was the kind whose ears prick up at the faintest rustle of money and couldn't force himself to ignore even a long chance when he smelled a con.

"Okay," he said a moment later. "Come on out. I'm leaving in a while but you can talk to my assistant if I'm gone."

"I'll be there quicker than a one-bean fart."

It was a lovely night. The moon was halfway up and three-quarters full, there was no breeze, and the summer evening scent was sweet enough to make the young fancy and the old foolish. In ten blocks I met one couple strolling arm in arm, who ignored me, and an old man taking his evening constitutional. He looked at me suspiciously, but responded in polite surprise when I wished him a good evening. If I'd asked for a match he'd have fainted.

Gyles' place was fairly modest for Park Avenue but was a good ways up from a lean-to. It had a broad porch with wide steps, white pillars, vine-covered brick walls and tall, fancy windows with leaded diamond-shaped panes. The light from inside was soft enough to come from candles.

I ambled up the long walk. Darkness obscured the porch until I was quite near and then I made out some-one sitting a little to the right of the front door. When I was almost to the first step a horse rose from the porch floor, made a noise like distant thunder and showed teeth not much longer than my thumb. Before panic reached my feet a husky voice said, "Down, damn it!"

"I never heard a horse growl before," I said in a voice so thin it squeaked.

The party sitting in the rocker beside the horse chuckled softly.

"He's only a dog."

"Begging your pardon, ma'am, but I've seen full-grown horses half that size."

"He's a mastiff. That's an Asiatic dog. They used to hunt wolves with them in olden times."

"What'd they do, trample them to death?"

I got the chuckle again. The monster rumbled and swung his head.

"What do you call him?" I asked.

"His name's Dammit. What's yours?"

"Carl Wilcox."

"You're looking for Julius, right?"

"Right."

"He's gone."

"I just talked with him—less than half an hour ago."

"Uh-huh. He was here then. Now he's gone. That's Julius all over."

"Why's he afraid of me?"

She shifted the rocker a little. "Because men are more dangerous than dogs."

While I was thinking that over she rocked the chair gently, and the dog, as if given a signal, settled on his haunches.

"You Mr. Gyles' wife?" I asked.

She laughed.

"His daughter?"

She laughed louder. The dog turned its massive head toward her and she shot her hand out, shouting, "Up, Dammit!" He lunged to his feet with a rumbling growl that rolled around in his barrel chest before spilling out at me. I stood frozen.

"Down, Dammit," she said softly, and the giant's rear end settled to the floor.

Fresh sweat covered me, making the night suddenly cold, and I felt happy only because I hadn't wet my pants. If that damned dog in horse's hide really came for me, I figured I'd empty everything like an iguana dumped in boiling water.

"You know the difference between an old maid and a bachelor girl?" she asked me, as though we'd just been discussing the weather.

"I don't think I ever heard." I hoped my voice sounded as casual as hers.

"A bachelor girl's never been married and an old maid's never been married or anything. I'm Gyles' bachelor-girl aunt."

"Oh. What's your name?"

"Olson," she said, and laughed again. The dog's head didn't turn, he just showed his teeth.

"You can call me Aunt Maude," she said.

"Okay. Did you know Kate Bonney?"

"She that woman with the boy's haircut that got herself killed? Sure. She came to see Gyles. He got real interested in her. He likes hard women. Especially hard women with money."

"Did she come around often?"

"Once. Six months or so ago. It was snowing that day. Snowed off and on most of that week. Piled up higher'n that step there. Dammit had a big time in all that snow, running around, rooting it up with his nose. Regular plow, only messy. You wouldn't expect a big dog like that to be playful, but Dammit's a regular kitten when he takes a notion. You want to pet him?"

"I'd as soon stick my hand in a lion's mouth."

"He won't bite if I don't say. That's a well-trained dog. Gyles trained him; used a length of two by four. He said nothing else'd get his attention. You like dogs?"

In front of Dammit I sure as hell wouldn't admit anything else, so I said sure, if they liked me.

"Do you know what Kate Bonney was after?" I asked.

"I think she was trying to prove she was a bastard child."

That threw me for a second before I asked, "How'd she figure to prove that now?"

"How'd I know?" She stuck her little finger in her right ear and jiggled it so hard I expected to hear a bone crack.

"Itches," she explained. "Ever see a dog with an itch in his ear? Nearly drives 'em crazy. I'd sure hate to be a dog."

"Yeah. Will Gyles be around tomorrow?"

"Hard to say. He comes and goes. Never know about Gyles. Always been like that. Wanted to be a lawyer from the time he was old enough to know better, went to war, got to be an officer; he was commissioned in the field, you know, from sergeant to lieutenant, just like that. I always used to say he should've stayed in, become a general, but he said you can't make general in a battlefield because they're never out there to get killed and need a replacement, so as soon as he got out he went to school learning law. He was a fine lawyer. Got into a big firm the day he graduated, made partner in just five years. Would've been a judge by now if it hadn't been for the trouble. Wouldn't have had the trouble if he hadn't been so impatient—"

"What was the trouble?"

"You don't know?"

"I'm from South Dakota, Maude, I don't know anything."

"My God, I thought even out there they read newspapers. It's a long story and I'm sick of it. Gyles was disbarred, that's the nub of it. Best lawyer in Minnesota, top of the heap, and now he spends his life poking around into secrets, so sick people can find ways to work other sick people. It's a sordid mess."

"Does he have an office downtown?"

She tried once more to reach the itch, which must have been in the center of her head, and after a moment tilted the chair back and sighed.

"He won't talk to you. You're wasting your time. Go home."

"My ma already figures my life's wasted. It won't help if I crawl back without what I came for."

"You still worrying about what your ma figures?"

"Not a lot."

"I should hope not. You're way too old for that. How old are you?"

"Old enough. How old are you?"

"Tit for tat, and go to hell. You want to sit down? I'd offer a drink, but then I'd have to get up and I don't do that till I have to."

"Have Dammit fetch."

"He's not *that* well-trained."

"Where do you pasture him?"

"He's a dog, not a horse, I already told you that. Of course he's no lap dog, but Gyles's gone a lot so he figures I need protection. Old Dammit's good at that. He could take your head off."

"I figure he could swallow me like a dog biscuit," I admitted.

"You bet." She reached over and patted the massive head.

As I sat down on the porch step near her feet a telephone rang somewhere deep in the house.

"You're not really a private detective, are you?" she asked.

"I don't know. I'm getting paid to be. You know your telephone's ringing?"

"It rings all the time. If it's important, they'll call back when I'm inside."

"I'll answer it for you."

"Not while Dammit's alive."

"I thought you said he was well-trained."

"He is."

The telephone kept ringing. I never break my neck to answer one, but I can't ignore them either, and the nagging persistency kept me from thinking of anything else. I took out my fixings and started building a cigaret.

The telephone stopped. Before I finished making a cigaret it began again.

"You've been in prison, haven't you?" she asked. For some reason the question didn't surprise me. I just looked at her and nodded. The telephone went silent.

"How'd people treat you when you got out?"

"Probably the same way people treated Gyles when he got disbarred. Lots of ways."

She scratched the dog's head and peered at me in the darkness.

"You have a wife before you got in trouble?"

"Before I got in *that* trouble, yeah."

"What trouble'd she leave you for?"

"If we're gonna tell each other the story of our lives, you're gonna have to start."

"I don't have any story."

"Okay, tell me about Gyles."

"I already have."

"How come you're here?"

" 'Cause he wanted me to come when his young wife walked out after he hit the skids."

"Did you know his wife?"

"I'd ought to—she was my little sister. Took Gyles away from me twenty years ago. She was a lot better looking and of course younger. That's what you men like. Young girls. You learn to want them when you're still snot-nosed kids and you never out-grow wanting the same kind of girls you knew first. You're mostly idiots."

"And women let us get away with it."

"That's right," she said, and laughed.

"So how come you came to him when she walked out?"

"It gave me some satisfaction, if you want to know the truth. Damned if I know why, now. But the funny part is, Gyles is a lot likelier fellow since his comedown. He's more real, if you can follow me. Before he was always running around, shaking hands, patting and kissing fannies, dressed to the nines. I'd tell him, back before my sister, for god's sake, come down off it once, but he didn't pay any attention to me except in bed. That was all that kept him human in those days—his hidden vice, so to speak. Marrying my sister spoiled all that. Then what he got was legal and accepted and I don't think he had any fun at all. I think that's why he stretched so far and finally got caught. He couldn't stand being perfect. Now he doesn't kiss anybody's behind. He comes and goes when he pleases and wallows in the mud now and then."

"And he's afraid to talk to some people."

"He's not afraid. He can't be bothered is all."

"The telephoner—is that someone else he can't bother to talk to?"

She pulled her hand back from the mastiff's head and rested it in her lap as she leaned back in the rocker. Somewhere in the distance a siren wailed and a couple of cars passed on the street below us. Slowly she leaned forward and came to her feet. The dog scrambled a second, gathering his long legs, scraped toenails on the porch floor and rose. His back was level with her waist.

"I'm tired," she told me. "I'm going in now."

"I've really got to talk with Gyles," I said, getting up. "He can't dodge me forever."

"He won't try. Don't make the mistake of pushing

him. I don't care how good a fighter you are, you'll find he's better, and he'll never raise a hand against you. You're not a bad fellow, Carl Wilcox, I can tell. Go home. You stay in Minneapolis and you'll get killed. That's the way it is. Good night."

Chapter XIX

Drizzling rain began to fall as I walked toward town and wet me clear down to my particulars by the time I reached the hotel. The ancient roomclerk gave me a look I foolishly assumed was sympathetic as he handed me my key. Up in the room I peeled down, dried myself with the huck towels folded by the water pitcher on the bureau and stretched out on the bed, bare-assed.

So far, I figured, the trip to Minneapolis was about as useless as a hike to Lil's whorehouse in Corden on Sunday. On the other hand, it was the first time in my life I'd gone anyplace with expenses paid, and that kept it from being a total loss.

I'd just finished my second cigaret when somebody mounted the steps and walked down the hall. Why that brought me to my feet is hard to say except I just knew it had to be some idiot coming to pound at my door and force me back into those wet pants.

And sure enough, the idiot pounded on my door.

I pulled on my icy pants, buttoned up and opened the door.

"My name's Gyles," the man said.

The voice on the telephone had given me a picture my visitor didn't match. Thin white hair flopped across his wide, smooth forehead. Ice gray eyes stared into mine with a look of flat indifference more threatening than hate. I glanced at his hands, expecting to see a gun, but they hung at his sides, pale and empty. His light gray suit was dry, well-pressed and virgin clean.

"You don't sound like Gyles," I told him.

"We'll talk," he said, and brushed past me so smooth and quick I let him get away with it and closed the door. He glanced around for a place to sit, then coolly removed my wet duds from the straight-backed chair, tossed them on the bed, wiped the seat with a handkerchief from his back pocket, and sat.

"What'd the old lady tell you?"

I picked my wet clothes from the bed and hung them on hooks behind the door.

"She told me her horse was a dog," I said.

"What'd she tell you about Kate Bonney?"

"She said Gyles had the hots for her. Is that right?"

He crossed his legs, fished a pack of Old Golds from his shirt pocket, shook a smoke loose, stuck it in his face and asked if I had a light.

"You got a spare smoke, I might."

He tossed the pack to me. I took a book of matches from the bureau, tossed them his way and sat down on the bed. He lit up and squinted at me through the smoke.

"The pack," he said, lifting his white hand.

As I tossed the pack he threw the matches only his pitch was weak and they almost reached the floor at my feet before I snatched them. When I straightened up I was staring into the barrel of a gun. It wasn't a very big gun, but the opening was wide enough to deliver more bad news than I could handle.

"What's that for?" I asked, leaning back.

"I just want you should know I'm not fooling around."

"I never figured you for a fooler, except for the name you handed me at the door."

"You know what Gyles looks like?" His eyebrows raised and I was glad to see it because that was as close as he'd come to showing human expression. It wasn't very close, more like a hint.

"I know what he sounds like."

He shook his head. "You know what a guy who answered the phone sounded like. You don't know it was him."

"You got a point." I wasn't really impressed, but never figured it paid much to argue with a dead-eyed man holding a gun.

"What'd the old lady tell you? And don't give me any more shit about her dog."

"She said Kate was at the house once and that she appealed to Gyles."

"What else?"

"She said Gyles wouldn't talk to me, that I was wasting my time and might get killed if I didn't go home. She told me the difference between an old maid and a bachelor girl and tried to make me think she slept with Gyles. Was she a good-looking kid?"

"She say what Kate hired Gyles for?"

"No. Don't you know?"

The gun muzzle moved like a waggled finger but not enough to miss me if he pulled the trigger.

"Don't get funny," he said. "I got a lousy sense of humor."

"You got a lousy line of reasoning, too. You know damned well I know you're not Gyles. If you were you'd go ask Maude what she told me. Gyles was a lawyer; he knows you don't need a gun to find out things or get things done. So what the hell's it to you what Maude told me?"

"I got to know if I need to knock her off, too, that's all."

I thought about that and wished I had more clothes on. Ma would be awfully upset to hear I'd died wearing nothing but unpressed pants.

"You're in luck," I said. "She didn't tell me anything, so you don't have to knock off anybody."

"You'd keep trying."

"Is it that easy to work out? Just a little information from a crapped-out lawyer?"

He shrugged. "Who told you about Gyles?"

"Why, you want somebody else to kill?"

"Maybe."

He said it thoughtfully.

A siren's wail echoed down the street and grew louder while my visitor and I stared at each other. When it growled to a halt in front of the hotel he came to his feet and darted toward the window just to my right at the head of the bed. I don't suppose he'd ever met a man quicker than himself, or maybe he was human and actually panicked for a moment. At any rate he came too close, the gun muzzle drifted and the next second he was on the floor with empty hands and a wrenched arm.

"Now," I said, giving him the view I'd been enjoying of the gun's muzzle, "how about we talk a little more only you answer the questions. Who the hell are you?"

He stared at me. The expression in his ice gray eyes
was the same as when he first entered, absolute indifference. Slowly he pulled himself together, stood up,
dusted his pants carefully with his left hand and hooked
his right thumb in his belt. I could tell it hurt him to
move, but he didn't wince or grimace.

Then, while I pointed the gun dead at his middle, he
calmly walked to the door, opened it, and left. I didn't
bother to threaten him. Obviously he knew I wouldn't
shoot.

I closed the door, shot the bolt and went back to look
out the window. A firetruck, gleaming in the rain threw
red lights across the wet pavement and sidewalk at the
far curb. A gaggle of rubberneckers hugged walls and
crowded doorways, hoping to see something exciting. I
opened the window and stuck my head out, thinking I
might see my visitor, but he didn't show. Then I remembered his suit hadn't been wet when he arrived. Either he was staying in the hotel, which seemed like
jerking the long arm of coincidence out of its socket, or
he'd been tipped off about where I was and arrived before the rain.

I pulled off my cold wet pants, sat on the bed and
broke the small pistol open. It was a thirty-two, five-
shot revolver with a stub barrel. There were two empty
shells in it. I sniffed the barrel and guessed it had been
used recently, but I don't really know about how you
tell that, so it didn't mean a hell of a lot beyond the fact
old dead-eyes didn't figure he'd need more than three
shells for me. Then I thought more about the whole visit and wondered if it was all a routine to plant the gun on
Wilcox.

Stark naked in a cool room I found myself sweating.

I dug a pair of dry shorts out of my ditty bag, put on dry sox, my wet pants, a dry shirt and soaked shoes and went to the door with the gun hanging heavy as an anchor in my rear pocket. It was so heavy I had to hold my britches up at the hip with one hand.

The hall was deserted as I hurried to the far west wing and found a window with a fire escape. It took some wrestling before I could get the window open and step outside. The rain had slowed to a fine mist and didn't bother me as I climbed to the roof two floors up. In a couple seconds I found a chimney, slipped the gun into it and let go. Two minutes later I was back in my sack.

I'd just begun studying the inside of my eyelids when hall boards creaked under a pair of heavy-footed characters who sneaked up to my door. After a second of silence there was a thunderous pounding.

"Open up! Police!"

"Come on in," I called, friendly as a whorehouse madam.

The door burst open and two harness bulls jumped in, separated, with guns in hands, and hit me with flashlight beams.

"Don't move!" yelled one. "Just hold it!"

"Sure," I agreed, and didn't so much as blink.

They pulled on the overhead light, jerked the covers off me and ordered me to sit up with my hands behind my back. One yanked me clear of the bed while the other snatched up the pillows, threw them on the floor and tipped the mattress over so it fell on the pillows.

When that didn't show what he was looking for he tried the bureau and looked into the empty pitcher sitting in the big white washbowl. After he'd gone through my bag and clothes, he turned to me with a nasty scowl.

"Awright, where is it?"

"Where's what?"

"Don't give me that 'where's what' shit. I'll bust your snout for you—you know what that's like, don't you?"

"I do, I do. But I can't tell you where anything is if I don't know what you're after—"

The guy who'd yanked me from the bed shoved me into the straight chair and cuffed my wrists behind me.

They went over the room again and then the yanker sat on the wrecked bed's edge and watched me while his partner went down the hall and checked the bathroom. When the partner returned the desk clerk came with him.

"Any rooms empty on this floor?" the big-mouthed cop asked him.

"No, all locked."

"Go check. Maybe this bum is a pick man."

His partner had my wallet and opened it wide to show the eighty plus dollars inside.

"We got a very flush bum, here," he said, "but nothing's got his name except this little ID card he's filled in. Where's your driver's iicense?"

"South Dakota doesn't issue them," I said.

"How about a license to carry a gun? They issue those in South Dakota?"

"I wouldn't know. I never carried one."

The desk clerk came back to say all the doors were still locked.

"Awright," said the big-mouthed cop. "Get into

your rags. We're taking you downtown."

"What's the charge?" I asked.

"Murder. Now move."

Chapter XX

City Hall in Minneapolis is a big pile of red rock with a clock tower and wide halls that echo when you walk down them. I read someplace that it cost a million dollars to build and I believe it. With a little bricking up of the bigger windows, it'd make a dandy castle. On the south side, where we entered, it even had a low wall and space between the sidewalk and building that could've been flooded for a moat.

They stuck me in the bullpen at first and it was damned strange to find myself sober in the midst of drunks. A bearded gorilla about half a head taller than me came over and stuck out his mit to shake, as if we were old buddies. I took his hand and he promptly tried to mash my knuckles. He had the vise for it, but I'd shoved my hand in hard so he couldn't grip the fingers and it annoyed him; he tried to clamp down with both hands. I did a dipsy-doodle, spinning to my left while swinging my arm over my head, and when he'd been spun around by the momentum I drove his wrist up between his shoulder blades, jerked my knee into his ass and slammed his head against the cell bars.

"Jesus," he said a while later when he came to, "you're a touchy little bastard, aren't you?"

"Not at all," I said, offering him a fresh rolled cigaret. "I always shake hands like that. It helps guys remember me."

About ten minutes later the two cops were back to take me out and lead me down a long hall to an unmarked door.

Bigmouth shoved me in and said I should sit. The door closed. I was alone. I looked at the gray walls and the wooden table in the center of the room with three chairs set neatly around it. took the one facing the door, sat down and rolled a cigaret. The butt was down to half an inch when the door popped open and a beefy plainclothesman swaggered in followed by a partner who could've been his twin except instead of being hairy like number one, he was bald.

"Carl Wilcox," said hairy, as he pulled back the chair on my right and sat down. "Thirty years plus four, alcoholic, ex-con, two-time loser, stick-up man and rustler. A very petty crook and bum. When'd you take up murder? Tonight your first?"

"No murder," I smiled. "If you know the record you know that's not my style."

"Oh, I know your record," he smiled back. His smile was lots brighter than mine. He had a fine dentist somewhere. "So tell me, if it wasn't for murder, what brought you to our town? What made us so lucky?"

I told him. While I talked to hairy, his bald partner walked behind me and stood quietly. I found it was hard to ignore him but even worse trying to hide how much it bothered me. I kept wishing I'd had sense enough to shove the chair back against the wall when I'd been alone.

"Where'd you stash the gun?" asked Baldy.

"The only time I ever had a gun was ten years ago

and that one was empty. It's in the record."

"You have any visitors at the hotel tonight?" asked Hairy.

"No." I felt pretty sure the deskman hadn't mentioned the phony Gyles.

"What'd you done if some mug came to your room and told you to leave town?"

"It'd depend on how convincing he was."

"What if he had a gun?"

"I'd leave town."

"You're just a real, easygoing, bank-rolled bum, right?"

"That's about the picture."

"You weren't so easygoing in the bullpen tonight," said Baldy.

"He didn't have a gun."

"How'd you know he didn't have a shiv?"

"It wasn't in his hand."

"He sure as hell didn't get much chance to reach for it," said Hairy. The way he grinned I guessed he wasn't crazy about the guy who'd tried to work me over. I also guessed the guy was a police stoolie.

Hairy asked where I'd spent the evening and I told him. While we were still talking about that, Baldy came from behind me, went out and closed the door.

By the time he came back, Hairy was asking me how I did rope tricks since for some reason my record included a mention of that. Before that he'd got the story about me booting an MP into a canal in France during the War. He seemed to enjoy that; even cops hate MPs.

Baldy called Hairy out and they had a short conference in the hall while I rolled and lit another smoke. Then Hairy opened the door again and tipped his head back.

"Okay," he said. "You're on your own."

"You talked to Maude?"

Baldy nodded.

"How's she doing?"

"How should she be doing?" asked Hairy.

"The cop that brought me in said something about murder. You asked me about murder. Since I'd been looking for Gyles, I figure something happened to him. If it did, Maude would be feeling down."

"She's down," he admitted.

The streets were wet, but the rain had stopped so I made the hike back to the hotel without getting my fresh shirt wet. My pants were still damp and cold and panhandlers ignored me. The deskman's head jerked as I came through the front door, but he made himself busy with something at the desk and didn't look me in the eye when I passed on the way to the stairs.

Before I'd gone halfway up the first flight the telephone rang behind the counter and the deskman called me back. He told me to take the call in the booth by the front door.

"You know who this is?" asked a husky voice. "Don't use any name—"

"I know."

"Come and see me. Now."

"Gimme fifteen minutes."

"Back way. I'll be waiting."

I walked over to the desk after hanging up.

"It was nice of you not to tell the cops I had a visitor tonight," I said.

"You didn't," he said and met my eyes defiantly.

"Right. I didn't have a telephone call either, did I?"

His eyes dropped. "I don't know about no telephone call."

"Fine. You're a prince."

I hiked at a good brisk pace until I reached Park Avenue and then shifted to a trot. A block from Maude's place I took to the alley. The sky was still overcast, and it was blacker than a witch's womb as I slowed to a steady walk. There were fences and lilac hedges lining the alley and only occasional, distant lights that winked dimly through branches or fence cracks. The gravel crunched under my feet.

The Gyles house stood second to the last on the block, and the garage was built next to the alley with a big double apron on the south side where the doors opened. I saw no light in the house and paused by the corner of the garage, trying to study the layout. Huge elms arched over the roof on each side, and after watching awhile, I saw there was a hedge up against the house in the rear with breaks for a cellar entrance and the rear door about six feet to the left. The lawn was clear on both sides. I waited until a car drove by on the street beyond the house. Its lights showed me no strange silhouettes and after taking a deep breath, I walked casually up to the rear door.

"Carl?"

"Yeah."

The screen door opened out and the next moment I'd slipped past Maude into a little vestibule that smelled of baked goods, spices and dry warmth.

She grasped my arm after she'd closed and locked the door.

"They've killed Gyles," she whispered. "They'll get you next, or me. Maybe both of us."

"Who killed him? How?"

"I'll tell you. I lied before. Gyles told me what he was up to. He always told me everything. I'm the only one he ever talked to. He wanted me to know how clever he was and knew I didn't judge him—like *she* did. That's what loving is, isn't it? When somebody just accepts you and you accept them the way they are—it's nothing to do with being young and smooth and stupid!"

She trembled and hung onto my arm as though it were a lifeline. We shuffled through the dark kitchen and slid into a breakfast booth by a south window. The blinds were drawn. Maude leaned across the table, still clutching my right arm.

"It happened twenty years ago," she whispered. "Over twenty. Gyles found they'd been living in a rented house in Hopkins—that's a suburb west of here—"

"Who?" I asked.

"Just let me talk. I'll tell you everything. The woman was friends with their neighbor—Simpson. Both women were alone a lot—they'd get together over coffee and talk about half the day—"

She spilled the story—hell, it was more like squirting—and I kept trying to slow her down or back her up so I could follow, but she'd only clutch my arm harder and keep talking. After nearly an hour she got up and made coffee in the dark.

"Don't need light," she told me. "Always get up at night and do it. Never turn on a light. Can't sleep but can't stand light in my eyes. Always been a night person. Hate birds—all their morning racket. Gimme an owl anytime."

We were both silent while the water heated in the coffeepot. Little red blips kept leaping up around the ring of blue flame, erratic as lightning. When she poured the coffee later it tasted bitter and black. She didn't offer cream or sugar.

After a couple of sips I pulled my arm free of her clutching hands and stood up.

"You're not leaving?" she asked. Her husky voice nearly cracked.

"Where's your dog?"

"I put him in the basement."

"How the hell's he going to protect you there?"

"I'm not sure I can control him. He's nervous. He knows I'm scared. I was afraid he'd attack you—"

"I thought he was trained."

"He is. Gyles could control him—but Gyles is never afraid."

"Well, if our killer comes through the basement, we'd ought to have plenty of warning—"

"Oh, yes!"

"I'm going to take a look around," I said. "You sit tight and don't worry."

She gave a bark of laughter. "What's to worry about. Who wants to live forever?"

I walked slowly through the big house to the front door and peered out through its oval glass toward the street. No cars went by. None were parked along the curb anywhere near. I returned through the living room, dining room and into the kitchen, where Maude still huddled in the booth over her coffee.

"It's a very quiet neighborhood," I said.

"Like the grave."

I walked through the rear vestibule and looked into the backyard. A loud scraping sound, from behind and below, froze me for a second. I wheeled and stared at the basement door in the vestibule. It was the dog, probably standing on his hind legs, scraping at the door below, putting his weight against it. I listened and heard the rumble from his deep chest. There was a moment of silence, then a crash as he threw himself at the door and scratched wildly at the panels. Then everything was quiet again.

I looked out the high window in the back door. Vague light from the city, reflecting against the overcast sky, made silhouettes in the broad yard and I wasn't surprised to see a figure slip around the far corner of the garage and move smoothly toward the house.

There was no bolt on the door; it was locked with a simple skeleton key.

I went back to Maude.

"You got any rope around?" I asked.

"Rope? I don't know. Might be some clothesline in the basement—"

"Let's go upstairs."

"Why? What's happening—what'd you see?"

"We got a visitor."

She slid out of the booth quickly, scraping her fingers on the table in her haste. It made a sound like the dog scratching the door below.

"Call the police," she whispered.

"You can try."

The telephone was in the dining room and she fumbled with it as I went toward the hall stairway and looked up into the darkness. Maude said, "Hello? Hello!" and clicked the hanger frantically.

"It's dead!" she cried.

"Yeah. Go upstairs, Maude. Better hurry."

"Oh, God," she said. "I don't mind getting killed, but I can't stand being hurt—"

As she scampered up the steps I looked around the

living room, spotted a small lamp near the hall door, turned it on and followed Maude.

The stairs ran up the south side and the first room at the top was the can. A right turn led into the master bedroom, which was evidently Gyles', next down the hall was Maude's and there was a third room beyond that. A railing ran around the stairwell top and there was a linen closet at the end of the hall. I got Maude into her room, pulled a bureau around to where she could shove it against the door when she was inside and suggested she push the bed and anything else she could handle in front of it.

"What're you going to do?"

"I'm not sure. Nothing that's gonna help that son-of-a-bitch, don't worry—"

"Don't worry? That's idiotic. You keep saying that and it's idiotic—"

"Okay, worry, but do it in the bedroom and barricade the goddamned door. Now!"

Once she was inside and shoving furniture I started scouting for war tools. The hall was hopeless and there was nothing really good in the bedrooms. The bathroom seemed equally bare until I looked at the tank lid. I hefted it and it was lovely—somewhere near ten pounds. I tucked it under my arm and walked down the hall around the stairwell and stopped, standing above the lower steps. The lamp I'd lit glowed, illuminating my view. I thought how lucky it was for me that things hadn't gone better for Gyles; with more money he might have had a bigger house and two stairways for me to watch. I rested the tank top edge on the iron railing which came up to my belt buckle.

There were no sounds from Maude's room and I wondered if she had piled enough stuff against the door but didn't dare go ask. The house was tomb still. I glanced out the open window on my left and listened for wind or the patter of rain, the sound of crickets or anything at all and only heard a gentle creaking from somewhere downstairs. Then the dog hit the basement doorway and began a frantic barking. Only it was more than a bark; it was nearer a roar. He was raging.

The killer was inside the house.

Gradually my hearing began to pick up as I concentrated, almost like a man's eyes begin to see in darkness that isn't complete. Despite the dog's noise, I sensed movement beyond the downstairs hall, lost it, thought I heard a creak, and then the dog was still.

A shadow fell across the first step below.

I inhaled slowly, gripped the tank lid with both hands and held tight as the shadow disappeared. He's going to turn off the light, I thought, and the next instant he was already a third of the way up the steps. I saw his head twisting as I jerked the heavy porcelain high and brought it down at the same time he whipped the gun around, and he caught the force of it full face. His shot thundered in the stairwell, and sent smashed crockery spattering like shrapnel. A piece sliced my jaw as I vaulted over the railing and went down on him with my body doubled up tighter than a bowling ball. He whooshed like a pricked balloon and went flat as I rolled backward into the front hall. I came up fast, not convinced he was out of business, but he only twitched once and slid down the steps like a smashed scarecrow.

Separating him from the gun was tough. The tank top had jammed his hand back, spraining his wrist and breaking his trigger finger, yet he still held on like a man in rigor mortis. His smashed face bled freely, turning his gray suit into something like a barn-painter's rag.

Maude slowly cleared her door after my all-clear signal and once it was open, stood staring at me.

"How do you know he was alone?" she asked.

Some people never want bad news to end.

"Because no one came to help him when he went down," I said.

She walked out into the hall and looked over the railing.

"Is that the one that killed Gyles?" she asked, without looking at me.

"I figure so. Have you got any friendly neighbors?"

She turned her eyes on me. Hate for the man below was still in her face. Her mouth was tight against her teeth, her skin seemed almost transparent. She looked old as death.

"Go next door and call the police," I said.

She looked at the gun I'd taken from the man.

"You call them. Just leave that with me. I'll watch him."

"No thanks. I still want to learn some things from this bird. Go call."

For a moment she hesitated, then she took a deep breath, turned, trudged down the stairs and passed the bedraggled wreck at the foot of the stairs without a glance.

"Don't let the dog up," I called.

She halted and for a moment I worried, thinking I'd only given her ideas, then she went to the front door and walked out.

I'd hoped that once the cops showed I'd get cleared in an hour or so and get back to the hotel for sack time, but of course I wound up back at city hall. Instead of the bullpen I got a private cell. Early in the morning I was in the interrogation room, being worked on by Hairy again. He said the gun I took off the killer hadn't been used on Gyles. It was a thirty-eight, not a thirty-two, and what'd I think of that?

I said I thought he must've been a two-gun man.

He said the desk man at the hotel had changed his story and now claimed I'd had a visitor and that visitor fitted the description of the fellow that wound up all bloody in Gyles' place. What'd I think of that?

I decided I'd better tell him about the gun I'd stashed in the chimney. To my surprise, Hairy was very pleased with me. He listened to my story twice, called in Baldy, got it again, grinned, shook his head and the two left, saying they'd see me later.

It was late afternoon when they visited me again. Hairy let me know he could really put my ass in a sling for obstruction, but since things had turned out fine once I came clean, he was going to be big about it all and let me go.

"I won't have to come back for the trial?"

"You just scoot back to South Dakota and forget you ever came to Minneapolis. And remember, you've been luckier than hell. This guy you creamed, Baltz, is strictly bad medicine."

"Baltz?" I recognized the name but couldn't place it.

"The mug in the gray suit. He's killed half a dozen guys we know about, probably more. These weren't just citizens either. These were mob boys, bootleggers. Old Baltz was the biggest heister in the state—used to hit trucks run by the mob."

So it was the bird the undertaker had told me about, the man who bullied the cop on the highway.

Hairy shook hands with me when we parted and suggested I stay in South Dakota from now on. It was a unique kind of bum's rush for me; I almost like it.

I ate dinner in a counter joint, got some change and went to a phone booth near the front door.

Maude sounded down at first, but my call seemed to shake her out of it a little and she asked if the cops had given me a hard time. I said they were fine.

"That's good. I told them you saved my life. I think that hairy cop believed me. He asked why I was talking to you and I told him some about our talk and you working for the people in that little town. But I have to tell you, he wants me to lie when I go to court against that killer."

"Yeah?"

"He says you wouldn't make a good witness because you've got a record. He says a defense attorney would chew you up on the stand and maybe they wouldn't be able to convict that fellow. I'm to say I dropped the tank lid on the man when he came up after me."

"Baltz'll love that. Wiped out by a woman. With a toilet-tank cover. He'll probably cut his own throat."

"That's fine with me. But is it going to bother you? Not getting the credit, I mean? After all, I do owe you my life. . . ."

"Don't worry about it. Hairy's right. Do as he says. Just keep thinking how much you'd like to have smashed the bastard and you'll be convincing."

"You won't be sore?"

"Hell, no, I owe you plenty, Maude. You gave me the answers I needed on the lake killing. I don't know what I can do with it, but at least I'm through running around in circles."

"Then it's all okay?"

"Everything's lovely."

"Okay. If you come back to Minneapolis, come around and see us. Dammit'll be nice once he gets acquainted."

I said fine and didn't bother to mention that I'd been invited to avoid Minneapolis by the police department.

Chapter XXI

It was dusk the next day when I got back to Aquatown, and I telephoned Avril from the bus depot. She invited me to the cabin.

"How about meeting me at the point west of the Wooden Palace?"

"Okay," she said.

I used money left from French's advance for a cab to the lake. It was dark when I got out and looked up at the big dipper and a good sprinkling of other stars all over the eastern sky. The pale glow in the west held off stars above the horizon.

The bald brow of the point looked deserted at first, but as I reached the top, Avril rose from the ground and walked slowly to meet me. When she offered her hands I took them in mine and we stood looking at each other in the half-dark.

"It seems like such a long time," she said. "I feel shy."

"I hope you didn't remember me as tall."

"I remember you well enough. I remember being here, too."

"Shall we look around for another couple?"

"Don't tease. You embarrass me." She kept holding

my hands, I guessed to keep me from starting
something.

"I've been to Minneapolis," I told her.

She tilted her head but said nothing.

"I talked with a man named Gyles. Kate hired him
to do some detective work for her."

"Oh?"

"Let's sit down."

She must have decided it was safe because I didn't
have a blanket along, and the next moment we were
seated, gazing out on the smooth, dark and star-
spangled lake.

I told her what had happened. Everything but what
Maude had told me the night Baltz attacked. Avril was
very interested in the action and my use of the toilet-
tank cover made her laugh. When she stopped laughing
she put her arms around me and we kissed. She said it
was all terribly exciting and that I must have a charmed
life, so of course I started making with the hands but
she stopped me.

"I want to," she said, "but I've got the curse."

I didn't swear. A long time ago I learned that
getting mad about the curse either makes a woman re-
sentful or ashamed, and I don't know which is worse
but both knock hell out of caring, and at the time I was
feeling awfully close to her.

"So let's have a week of messing around—give it a
good buildup—"

"No, I'd go crazy. You want me to do something?"

"No, just save up for me. I wouldn't want to go
alone."

That about made her purr and I was proud, if
frustrated.

"What was Maude like?" she asked.

"Now why'd you ask me that?"

"Well, wasn't she Gyles's mistress? Aren't mistresses always sexy?"

"I thought of her more as his mother."

"Was she really so old?"

"I don't know. Never saw her in good light."

"Would you have made a pass if the dog hadn't been there?"

"The second time around, the dog was in the basement."

"But then she was afraid. And she was talking, wasn't she?"

"She talked."

"What'd she tell you?"

I stretched back flat and cradled the back of my head with my hands on the cool grass. She lay beside me, close and warm on her belly and leaned her face over mine.

"She said Gyles was hired to find out who Kate's real father was. Kate had worked out the timing, she'd dug up the fact that her mother was in the Cities at a time right for Kate to have been planted. And she learned by accident about this guy who'd worked for old Timmerman, and this employee had gone off at the same time. Gyles managed to fit it all together, only he was such a tricky character I'm not sure I believe a damned thing he claimed even if Maude was positive he had the straight goods. And God knows she should have been able to tell when Gyles was leveling. Anyway, now I think I know what happened and who did what to who and made Kate. But I don't have a particle of evidence and there're more loose ends in this case than you'd find in a Chicago whorehouse."

"So what're you going to do now?"

"Well, right now I'd like to know does Ryder have any hoodlum friends who handle rough stuff for him?"

"Ryder? What's he got to do with all this? You're not going to tell me *he's* Kate's real father?"

"No. But I think he put a couple guys on me after I had my first talk with you. I think he's a little crazy where you're concerned."

She twisted around and sat up beside me.

"I don't understand. I don't see what Ryder's got to do with this Kate thing?"

"As far as I know, there's no connection at all. But two guys have been following me that don't fit into anything but my notion that Ryder's afraid of competition and he's tried to squelch it—meaning me."

"Well, he does know a lot of people—and they're not all nice. I suppose he could find someone who'd do him a favor for a little money. . . ."

"You know who they might be?"

"No, I'm afraid not."

"Look, baby, it's kind of important. These sons-of-bitches have tried to kill me twice. That's more than a little favor."

"I can't believe Ryder'd do anything *that* bad."

She was trying to convince herself of something she didn't quite believe.

"Okay. How about you help me make sure?"

Her head jerked nervously. "How?"

"Just let him know, sort of by accident, where he could find me alone."

She bowed her head and sat silently for a moment. Finally she looked at me.

"What do you want, revenge?"

"I want those bastards off my back."

"I'll take care of it," she said. "That is, if he's really the one behind it."

"Fine."

I got up, helped her to her feet and we kissed.

"What're you going to do next?" she asked.

"Go talk with Sig French."

"Is *he* Kate's father?"

"That's what Gyles told Maude."

"Then certainly he wouldn't have killed her."

"Doesn't seem like, does it? But you'd hardly figure he'd cut off two of his daughter's fingers either, would you?"

"Oh, my God." She shuddered. "It's too sordid to believe."

"Well, cheer up, maybe none of it's true."

Chapter XXII

Sig answered my knock. His jaw dropped as he opened the inner door and saw me, then he managed to grin, moved the screen aside and reached for my hand like a huckstering politician.

"Well, as I live and breathe. If it isn't Carl Wilcox. How the hell are you, you old son-of-a-gun. How'd it go? Come on in. Lorna's going to want to hear this."

He kept chattering wildly as we moved through the kitchen and into the living room. Lorna, still in black, sat on the couch beside the fireplace, which had been cleaned out with a thoroughness that suggested it'd never know another ash. Her cold gray eyes lifted from her knitting and took me in calmly.

"Well," she said, jabbing the needles without pause, "how'd you find the big city?"

"It was easy. They had it built all around the depot where I got off the train. Couldn't miss it."

She rewarded me with a smile colder than a new popsicle.

"Well, I take it you were successful. Certainly you're in good spirits."

"Yeah. Actually I didn't expect to find you folks still here. Thought you'd be long gone."

"We couldn't sell the cabin," said Sig. "There's some nonsense about the will. Legal crap. It's all right with me, though, I haven't had a vacation in six years."

There was an awkward pause I did nothing to ease. When Sig started to prattle I interrupted him rudely.

"I've got a friend who might be interested in buying the place when things get squared around. How much property's included?"

The idea of a sale brightened him up. "It's a double lot. A hundred and twenty feet of lakeshore and it runs about two-fifty back to the access road. Good land, clean and level—"

"Let's go out and look it over."

His enthusiasm faded, he glanced toward Lorna doubtfully and back at me. "What about your trip to Minneapolis?"

"I got nothing solid. Besides, I'll have to talk with Lieutenant Baker before I know what it all means."

"Well, now, that's kind of high-handed, Carl. I'm paying for your time. Seems like the least you could do is tell us what you found out."

"Later. Let's go look around."

Lorna's eyes narrowed, but she nodded when he looked her way and we went outside. Sig hung back, like a kid following his old man to the woodshed. I walked slowly toward the beach. When we were both on the sand I turned toward him.

"Your man Baltz is in a Minneapolis hospital, under police guard. He killed a guy named Gyles. He tried to kill me."

Sig's hands raised involuntarily, as if he expected a blow. When I made no move he lowered them slowly and cleared his throat.

"Who was this—what—?"

"Baltz. You know him. You hired him, you son-of-a-bitch, don't give me this innocent crap."

I took a step toward him and again his hands jerked up and he stumbled backward.

"Wait!" he cried. "Carl, what're you going to do—?"

"I'd ought to stick your face in the sand and sit on your head, but that'd only land me in the pokey again so all we'll do is talk. If you talk."

He recovered his balance, pushed his hands down at his sides and gathered his dignity.

"Why're you mad at me? What've I done to you?"

"Oh, nothing serious—just tried to get me murdered. But don't worry. I won't hold a little thing like that against you. What makes me mad is all the other lousy things you've done. It's going to take some time to prove them, but I'll goddamned well take the time, and if I can't get your ass in court I'll make sure everybody knows what an eight-angled asshole you are."

"You can go to jail for libel," he told me.

"That'll do you a fat lot of good, pal. Everybody'll still know, and you can't handle that, Sig. You want to be the beardless Santa Claus, loved by all. How do you think people'll treat a man who chopped up his own kid and then murdered her—for money?"

"Listen—it wasn't like that at all—it's not as simple as you make it sound, Carl—I didn't have any choice—it was—"

"You didn't have any choice but to lay your boss's wife, kidnap the kid you planted and finally strangled to keep her from finding out you were her real father? Don't tell me. It was a curse, right?"

"In a way, yes! Look—it's a long story. Lorna'll be out looking for us any minute now. She doesn't trust me out of her sight any longer than that. Listen, I'll tell you, I want you to understand, but you've got to let me tell it all. You can't understand anything if you don't know it *all*. . . ."

"From what I know so far, I'm not sure I've got the belly for the whole story."

He was right about Lorna, she came out the back door and called for him. He answered, saying he'd be right in, not to worry.

"I'll talk to you tomorrow," he told me.

"Okay. Come to Corden."

"No. Absolutely not. It's got to be in the open somewhere, a place where nobody can hear but you. I can make you understand. You're an understanding man. But I'm not going to have eavesdroppers."

"Fine. And I'm not going to have bushwhackers. What kind of an idiot do you take me for? Just because Baltz is in the hospital doesn't mean you've run out of hired killers."

He shook his head and lifted his right hand.

"Carl, you've admitted you've got no proof of any of these wild claims you've made. You want to know what's happened and I can tell you. There's no reason for me to want you killed. Just listen and understand. I didn't kill Katie, I honestly didn't. I couldn't have done that, no matter what. . . ."

"Okay. Meet me in front of city hall. I'll pick you up in my truck and we'll take a ride. You'll be able to see I'm alone and I'll be sure you can't set up an ambush."

He didn't like it and we hassled awhile, but my plan was finally accepted. I walked back to the house with

him and waved at Lorna who stood in the doorway as I
climbed into my truck.

Her cold eyes watched me without fear and it made
me wonder.

Chapter XXIII

"To understand any of it," said Sig, "you'd have to know about Ellie Timmerman. Her maiden name was Wallace and she was the last of about a dozen kids in a middle-class Catholic family. Just to look at her you'd think she was the last woman on this earth that a dried-up banker like Timmerman would marry. She was so round where you want it that you'd have to squeeze her any time you saw her. Just juicy, you know the kind?"

I guessed I did.

He shook his head and stared through the truck windshield at the graveled road before us, which stretched across the rolling prairie and thinned to a point on the horizon.

"Marrying a woman like that'd be a sinful act for most people in South Dakota. Not decent. You couldn't look at her without lascivious notions. . . ."

His thoughts left the truck and I brought him back, asking how old she was when he met her.

"Less than thirty. Looked about twenty, which is what I was. Well, actually, I was more like twenty-three. There was this big party Timmerman threw just after I'd started working in the bank. She was in the re-

ception line near the door and when she shook hands
with me and looked into my eyes I felt a jolt. Honest to
God, it was like an electrical shock. She looked at me as
if she knew right then that I wanted every woman I
saw, and she was letting me know she'd be the best there
ever was. I went through the rest of that evening in a
regular funk. I didn't have the nerve to drift by where
she stood talking with guests. I was positive if she
spoke a word to me I'd go tongue-tied and witless. But
I kept looking her way and almost every time, her
eyes'd meet mine. Once, when that happened, her eyes
dropped to my mouth and she licked her lips, very deliberately, with her pink tongue while she was looking at
me.

"I dreamed about her all night. The next time I saw
her I was in the bank. She'd been to see her husband,
for shopping money or something, and when she came
out of his office she passed my desk, smiled at me and
said, 'Good day, Mr. French.'

"I tell you, Carl, I couldn't even speak. I'd been
thinking about her so much and having dreams, and I
know I turned red and I was positive that somehow
she knew about my dreams and was laughing at me.
That made me mad. I told myself she looked lots older
in daylight and she was too fat. But my mind was full of
her. I did feel like she'd put a spell on me. . . .

"Anyway, next I saw her at the drugstore. It was a
Saturday early in spring. I'd gone to buy razor blades
and there she was, picking up a prescription for old
Timmerman. She smiled at me and I asked, right out, if
I could buy her a soda. I didn't stutter or blush, just
came right out with it. She lifted her eyebrows and said,
'Why not?'

"God, I was excited. We sat there at the fountain

where anybody in town could've seen us and I talked to her like a madman. I don't remember anything else in the store—not who waited on us, what flavor she ordered—all I know is she watched while I talked and laughed when I cracked wise and, Carl, I just took off. I told her about things that happened in the bank, I mimicked customers I was sure she knew. I even mimicked Timmerman and the more I went on the more delighted she seemed. I don't know how long we were there. Maybe it was only twenty minutes, maybe an hour, but I was never wittier or more handsome in my life. When she got up to leave she told me I was quite the most charming young man in town.

"We met the next Saturday. It rained. I was awfully afraid she wouldn't show up. After all, why should she? But she did: Only this time, things were different. I noticed that the fellow running the fountain was paying too much attention, and there were people at a little table that I'd seen in the bank, and it wasn't as easy to make Ellie laugh. After a while, when the fellow was over serving the table people, I asked Ellie if she'd have lunch with me the next Saturday at a little restaurant down the street. She gave me a long look, licked her lips and asked, 'What are you building up to, Mr. French?'

"Now, honest to God, Carl, I *knew* she was going to say something like that. I *knew* it! That was her style. And I'd rehearsed what I'd say and I said it exactly. I said, 'I'm afraid to think, let alone say.'

"She laughed, turned to look around, touched my knee with her fingertip and said it was a date. 'One o'clock. Don't forget.' "

Once he was into his story, Sig was so carried away he couldn't bear to skip a detail. I tried to crowd him along at first, but he ignored me and I wound up letting him ramble. It was damned obvious that Ellie'd been the world's greatest little cockteaser and had no intention of getting herself involved with a twit like Sig, but before long, Sig was smart enough to get himself out of the bank and into sales with an oil company where he began making money. Ellie started taking him seriously then.

"I knew I was getting somewhere," Sig told me smugly, "when she began getting jealous about Lorna. She'd ask questions about how we got along in bed. I claimed we didn't do anything. That wasn't so, of course, because when Ellie'd get me all worked up I'd go home and practically rape Lorna. I'd imagine—you know? It wasn't easy because Lorna was—well, she didn't have the juiciness of Ellie. I mean, she was a good wife, made fine meals, served 'em on time, kept a nice house, didn't pick at me—not in those days. Anyway, Ellie's asking questions got me more excited than ever. I'd never known a woman that'd dream of talking about people in *bed*. And I'd ask her, what about her and old Timmerman and she'd tell me not to be ridiculous, that he was an old man who never even thought of touching her that way. Of course I believed her. I thought he *was* ancient. That's funny, you know. He was no older then than I am now. Maybe younger. Jesus."

"Sig," I said, as he sat there remembering, "you remind me of a story about the man who found the whorehouse so full only the white-haired madam was available, and he agreed to bed her when she said there might be winter in her hair but there was summer in her heart. So they went at it and pretty soon he said to her, 'There may be winter in your hair and summer in your heart, but if you don't get more spring in your ass we're gonna

be here till fall.' Now, Sig, how about you get to the goddamned climax before the leaves fall.''

"Well, nothing really happened between us but kisses
and some petting until the oil company had a convention
in the Cities. It was early December and I got the idea
that Elllie should make a Christmas shopping trip at the
same time. Lots of South Dakota swells did that every
year, the women, I mean. It didn't take a lot of coaxing.
By that time we'd worked each other up till we were both
ready to bust. Anyway, it worked out just lovely. She
went to the Andrews Hotel and I was with the convention at the Nicollet, just a couple blocks away. When it
came right down to the night, I was scared to death. I
figured the fellow I was rooming with might blab to the
wrong people if I was gone late, or somebody might
spot me going into the Andrews, you know, all that
stuff. But it turned out perfect. All of a sudden there we
were, Ellie and me, in a hotel room with a bed and everything. I'd brought a bottle of champagne only I
hadn't figured a way to cool it and Ellie shocked me by
calmly ordering a bucket of ice from room service. They
brought it up and I hid in the bathroom while she
talked to the bellhop and I was awed by her calmness
and a little scared of her. She was so goddamned in control! She showed me how to open the bottle, using a
towel over the top after you twisted off the wire and
then working the cork with your thumbs till it popped.
Then we sat there, her on the bed and me on the only
chair after she'd turned the gaslights so low they were
like birthday-cake candles. We sipped the champagne
and she asked what I was going to do next. I was so
stupid, at first I thought she meant about my work and
the two of us, but no, she wanted me to say exactly how
I was going to make love to her. She wanted me to talk

all about it. Well, I started to say how I'd kiss her and then take her clothes off and then we'd get in bed and do it and she said that wasn't very great, didn't I want to kiss her all over and look at her when she was naked, wouldn't I like her to walk around with nothing on and wouldn't I like to have her do things to me. . . ."

The memory made him sweat with excitement as he sat there in my dilapidated truck and stared out at the sunburned prairie that stretched for miles around us. I expected him to tell me how they'd finally come to an earthquake climax with flooding juices and screaming ecstatics, but he actually told me he came too soon and all of Ellie's frantic efforts to revive him only made his wong wilt like a waterless daisy. Ellie wept at first, then raged and he finally left the hotel room without even finishing the champagne. I got the notion that this waste of his first champagne upset him almost as bad as not being able to get another hard-on.

"So later she turned up pregnant?" I said.

He nodded wearily.

"Well, at least you got it in. Some don't get that far."

"She called me old 'Single-Shot Sig,' " he said thickly, and his eyes watered.

"It happens to the best of us."

"I'll bet it never happened to you."

I smiled wisely. Somehow I couldn't feel kindly toward him.

"How'd Lorna find out?" I asked.

"She heard that Ellie'd gone to the Cities when I was there at the convention. She'd been suspicious before, so it didn't take much to get her thinking. She'd made cracks clear back when I was at the bank about how Ellie flirted with every young fellow in town and that she was a shameless hussy who even made eyes at me. But to tell you the truth, what really made things bad was that Lorna was pregnant. You know how women get when they're pregnant?"

"Big."

"They get sensitive and broody. All that peaceful Virgin Mary motherhood is crap. She got suspicious and bossy. There was no pleasing her, and of course she was sick every morning."

"You got to hating her, eh?"

"No. I just felt guilty as hell. You know, here I'd got her that way, probably some night when I did it while thinking of Ellie, and then Ellie turned out to be worse than a whore who tried to destroy me. I tell you, Carl, that's what she tried to do. She made me feel like I was *nothing* after she went and got me so worked up I was crazy out of control."

He shuddered, cut off the flow, folded his thick arms and leaned back in the seat. When he closed his eyes a tear rolled down his broad left cheek. He didn't notice it.

"So you moved away," I said.

"Well," he said defensively, "it was the only thing to do."

He wiped his face and lowered both hands to the seat.

"I got a job in Minneapolis, still working for the oil company. For a while I thought it'd turned out fine, and I think it would have. I made a lot of new friends—I never had any trouble making friends. People always liked me, and during the last part of her pregnancy, Lorna perked up. I figured everything was turning out for the best. Only a week after the baby came, he died. Something wrong with its heart, they told us. Lorna went into a regular blue funk, didn't talk, cook or do housework. And the first thing she said

when she finally started talking was it wouldn't have
happened—the baby dying—if I hadn't gone and lain
with another woman. She said it was Ellie's fault. Oh,
she was generous with the blame, she gave me plenty,
but mostly she laid it on Ellie because she was older and
should've known better. She said I was too naive to be
responsible. Then one day we were shopping and ran
into a couple we'd known in Aquatown. The fella'd
worked in Timmerman's bank with me, and he talked
about how the Timmermans had had this beautiful baby
and there was talk in town that it wasn't really his. Jesus,
I could've killed him."

"I expected an explosion when we got home, but
Lorna didn't say a word. Just pulled in like a turtle
caught in traffic."

"I'm mixed up," I said. "How was Timmerman related to you?"

"He was my mother's uncle. They came from New
York state. The family claims they moved west in covered wagons. Old Timmerman bragged that he walked
all the way beside the wagon, carrying a rifle. I never
believed him, not for a minute."

He wanted to talk about the family some more, but I
managed to head him off and steer him back to Lorna.

"We had pretty normal times for a few years after
that. I worked hard and made quite a bit of money and
Lorna took care of the house and got into church work.
We probably seemed like anybody else to our friends.
After a while we even began sleeping together and then
Lorna got pregnant. If that hadn't happened every-
thing might've been okay. I mean, before the pregnan-
cy she only turned moody when we got Christmas cards
from Aquatown, or somebody sent a birthday greeting.
Anyway, the second baby was stillborn. Lorna quit the

church and shut me out. The company cut my territory
so I wasn't making as much money, and finally it got so
I didn't want to go home and I drank with the guys and
one day I was fired."

He glanced my way to see if I was grasping the depth
of his tragedy and I gave him the long face he needed.

"When I finally worked myself up to tell Lorna I'd
been fired, she didn't even blink. For a while I didn't
think she even understood what I'd told her. Jesus, I
can't tell you how awful it was. Because, you see, in
spite of everything, I really loved Lorna. I mean, we'd
been through all this together and she knew all about me
but was still mine. . . ."

"So what happened?"

"It came to a head on a Thursday night. By God,
I'll never forget that. I had an interview with this son-
of-a-bitch who'd found out why the oil company fired
me. He spent a good half hour telling me about the evils
of demon rum and why nobody else would hire me and
finally why *he* wouldn't hire me. For a time there he had
me thinking I'd get the job because he figured I'd
work for nothing. Hell, I was ready to at that point. I
walked out of there absolutely whipped. I didn't have
gumption enough left to swat a mosquito. Just enough
to go for a few drinks before facing Lorna."

He stared through the windshield at a tumbleweed
which rolled across the scorched prairie and piled into a
stack of mates by a barbed-wire fence. Cowpies scattered over the stubble grass had been baked and
bleached until they looked like tan, flat stones.

Sig took a deep breath and went on.

"Lorna didn't criticize when I came in, stinking of
booze and walking carefully to keep from staggering. As
a matter of fact, she apologized, saying she'd put the

meat loaf in too early and she was afraid it'd be a little dry but we could fix it with catsup. She had it spiced and there were mashed potatoes with butter and salt and pepper and Harvard beets. I always liked Harvard beets. We ate without any talking, and when we were through she cleared the dishes away and poured coffee for us and sat down across from me, leaned her elbows on the table and said, 'I've a plan.'

" 'For what?' I asked. She was all of a sudden so confident and friendly that it got to me and I began to revive. Or maybe it was having eaten. Anyway I looked at her and had this wonderful feeling that things were going to be all right after all. She still believed in me.

" 'We're going to get some money,' she said.

"I asked her from where.

" 'From your great-uncle. And at the same time, we'll punish his bitch-wife.'

"Then she told me her plan. We were going to kidnap Timmerman's daughter, Kate. Really my daughter, which made it all right. We'd go to Aquatown and pick her up, wait a couple days, then send a note demanding ransom.

"Now, you're probably not going to believe this, Carl, but so help me God, it's the absolute, pure as snow truth. I guessed that what she really had in mind was stealing the kid for ourselves. She'd lost two babies, you know, and she wanted one the worst way, and I figured she thought Ellie's child was really ours and she made up her mind to have it. I suppose I kidded myself because that's what I wanted. I've always been crazy about little girls and wanted one of my own. It just killed me knowing Ellie had this little girl by me and I couldn't have any part. . . ."

Another tear rolled down his cheek and his talk choked off. I discreetly looked out the window on my left.

"I never believed it'd really happen," his voice was a whisper. "She said we'd go to town and take Katie from her bed when the Timmerman's were out. Lorna'd been reading Aquatown newspapers and had talked with old friends and had learned all about the house and the Timmermans' habits and how they were with the little girl. The daughter of one of our friends used to babysit for Kate, so it just happened to come up that Kate always had an afternoon nap on the sunporch. All the time we were driving back to South Dakota, and even up to when I was sneaking onto the sunporch, I was positive something'd happen to save me, but everything went exactly like Lorna planned. It was just meant to be, you know.

"Katie was wonderful. I put my hand over her mouth right away and she never panicked or cried. As soon as I could, when we were in the car, I talked to her. We kept her blindfolded all the time, and I always whispered when I talked, trying to disguise my voice. I used the singsong talk you hear from Norskies around here. I promised she wouldn't be hurt and we'd take the blindfold off as soon as we could, and I bought her an ice-cream cone in Bristol, near the border. She said she'd never had a cone so late before and it was hard to eat when you couldn't see, but she did all right. She was very brave, even excited. She told me once that she was having an adventure.

"Lorna's original plan was that we weren't going to talk with Katie at all hardly, but real early I could see the more I said to her the less nervous she was and there was no advantage in having her frightened, so

what the heck? For a while I thought even Lorna was
charmed by Katie. I'll tell you, Carl, that was the most
lovable little girl anybody ever saw. But Lorna wouldn't
talk to her and when she wanted to ask questions, she
had me do it. Like she wanted to know how she felt
about her parents. Lorna thought there was something
strange about Katie's not being more upset about being
taken away from her home. At first Katie said she
thought they were fine, but she was clever enought to
figure out in no time what we really wanted her to say so
she got critical. You could tell she had some trouble
saying bad things about her mother, but with old Timmerman it was different. He was distant and uneasy
with her.

"Timmerman was that kind of man. He didn't want to
know anything or anybody that'd make him feel uncomfortable. It makes me laugh the way people kowtow to
a bastard like that because he owns a bank and dresses
like a corpse in a casket and looks down his nose at us
poor slobs. He never knew anything. Never understood
women. Hell, I doubt he was ever a kid. He was probably born in a suit with a gold watch on a chain across his
vest and his hair slicked down over his balding dome.
He must've been *born* president of the bank. He didn't
have brains enough to start anything on his own—"

"You really hated him, didn't you?" I said.

He turned to meet my gaze and stared for a moment,
thoughfully. Before answering, he looked out at the
pasture around us.

"No. I never hated anybody. I just wanted everybody to like me. He didn't. When I worked in his bank
I figured he was a stuffed shirt, but I didn't feel much
of anything about him. He was just there, sort of like the
clock on the corner outside, part of the building, you

know? I never could think of him as Ellie's husband.
He was more like her father. You know how old folks
seem to the young. I mean, except for parents, they
just don't count except as bossy bastards who keep
getting in the way. They're never really people to you."

"How about Kate? Wasn't she more of a doll than a
kid you'd fathered?"

"I suppose she was until we'd had her with us
awhile."

The brightness of the prairie bothered his eyes and he
blinked and squinted before going on.

"The waiting passed like forever. You see, Lorna figured we'd build up tension on Ellie so when she learned
that Katie was alive, she'd be so relieved and excited
she'd do anything to make old Timmerman shell out.
She wanted two hundred thousand dollars. I told her
that Timmerman couldn't come up with all that, and she
said he could so, he ran a bank didn't he? That's where
the money was. She hadn't mentioned any fortune like
that before we stole Katie. She'd just talked about
enough to set us up comfortably, give me a chance to
start a business out west. She had the notion of Denver
for some reason. I was more for California. But when
she started talking about two hundred thousand dollars
I could see she didn't just want money, she wanted to
wipe out Ellie by making Timmerman an embezzler. I
really got scared about then, because I saw for the first
time how full of hate Lorna was and it came to me that
her hate was strong enough for her to kill Katie.

"I tried to argue with her, saying if we asked for a
reasonable amount, Timmerman'd raise it quick and
the whole thing'd be cleaned up in no time without fuss,
but she wouldn't hear of it. She said I was small-

minded and what's more, I cared more about Ellie and her bastard kid than I did about her. I mean, she raved. It just scared me spitless."

Sig hunched over in the truck seat and squeezed his hands together until the knuckles turned white.

"I got Katie to write a note to her mother telling her everything was fine and please would they do what Mr. King asked and she'd be home soon. I used the name Mr. King. Then we fixed up a demand note to go with it out of letters taken from the Minneapolis Journal. Lorna did that. When I read it, Jesus, my blood *froze*. I got that kind of headache you have when you're real hot and suddenly drink something awfully cold—have you had that? It hits you between the eyes, like a hammer. The note said that every day after the tenth, a finger would be cut from Katie's hand and mailed to them."

Sig wiped his sweating face with a handkerchief and shook his head when I offered him a smoke. I rolled one for myself and got it lit before he started talking again.

"You catch on to what she was doing, don't you?" he said, looking my way out of the corner of his eye. "She was punishing Ellie *and* me."

I nodded. "How'd you get the note to the Timmermans?"

"Just dropped it in the mail."

"Then what?"

"Two days later, Lorna telephoned. I don't know how she disguised her voice, or if she even tried. For all I know she might've wanted Ellie to know who she was and dared her to do something about it. It'd have been like her at the time. Anyway, she told Ellie to get the

money together and then we'd call back and arrange for
the pickup. I stayed with Katie while Lorna made the
call."

"Where'd you keep her?"

"We stayed at a farmhouse in Minnesota that be-
longed to an old uncle of Lorna's. He'd gone broke on it
and was in a city apartment when he died and left it to
us. We couldn't sell it. Nobody wanted farms then, at
least not that one. Katie's room was upstairs in back. I
went up and talked to her when Lorna was gone. I always knocked on the door and told her it was me and
she'd put on the hood like I'd told her, and then I'd go
in and we'd sit in the little room and talk. Outside you
could hear the prairie wind all the time. Katie said it
sounded like ghosts howling at night. When she talked
about home she mostly told me about her cat named
Cousin Gray. She called him Cuz. She said he was big
and gray and very lazy except when he chased squirrels.
Katie worried about him a lot because her mother
wasn't too fond of cats and her old man didn't like 'em
at all, and she was afraid they'd forget to feed Cuz and
not let him in late at night. Katie always heard his meow
and went to let him in, no matter the hour. So when
Lorna got back from making her phone call, I went out
and found a kitten for Katie. It was little and orange
with tiger stripes and a kink in its tail. I suppose it'd got
caught in a door somewhere. Katie named him Ike. I
fixed up a cat pan and bought some Red Heart dog food
and let her feed him. That was the best time of all. She
was so tickled!"

"So," I said, "up until you chopped off her fingers
you were all having a cozy time?"

He shrank in the seat. "She loved me," he whispered. "I was real good to her. Nobody else grownup

had ever sat down and listened to her and told her things
a little girl likes to hear—"

"Like what a bastard her father was?"

"I did tell her it was Timmerman's fault we couldn't
take her home," he admitted. "Later—when I had to
hurt her—I said it'd never have happened if he hadn't
been such a tightwad. Jesus, it was true! That tight son-
of-a-bitch didn't make a move. Till Ellie began to lose
her mind after they got the first finger."

"Well, what the hell, it wasn't even his own daughter," I said. "And to pay you off he had to steal from
his own bank. It meant wiping himself out. Didn't you
ever think of that?"

"Aw, bullshit! Rich ones like Timmerman, they look
after each other. Like goddamned royalty. They'd have
bailed him out if he'd asked. You aren't gonna make me
cry for that fat slug. I cried for Katie and me and for
what it all did to Lorna. She was a nice girl once. . . ."

Yeah, I thought, *wouldn't it be pretty to think so.*

Sig leaned forward with his head in his hands and
rocked back and forth. I finished my cigaret, butted it
out in the ashtray and looked over the rusting truck
hood at the sunburned prairie.

"People've always liked me," he said. "I'm a nice
guy. That's been my real trouble, you know, being the
kind that wants love. Always trying to please everybody. You're like that, Carl, everybody likes you and
what's it got you? A lot of trouble, that's what."

"The trouble I've had, old buddy, is a pimple on a
gnat's ass to what you're in."

He shook his head. "It was too long ago. They can't
do anything to me now; there's a statute of limitations or
something like that. I read about it once."

"You think people you know are still going to think

you're a nice guy when they hear?"

"Listen," he said earnestly, "even Katie forgave me. If she did, why should anybody else care?"

"If she forgave you, why'd you have her killed?"

"I didn't! Didn't have a thing to do with it—"

"You didn't hire Baltz to stop her private eye in Minneapolis and strangle Kate at the lake?"

"Never!" His eyes were wide and brimming.

"So it was Lorna."

He blinked, tears ran down both cheeks and he turned his face away. "I never thought of that," he whispered.

"I'll bet. What made you think Kate forgave you. Are you trying to tell me she found out before she was killed that you were her father!"

"She'd guessed," he said after taking several seconds to control his voice. "I expect it came slow, but over the years we'd see her now and again. She came to visit, you know, and we'd be talking and she'd look at me real funny and it was especially noticeable one night after I'd been telling a story about a cat we'd had. I think she remembered my voice, the way it'd sounded to her behind the hood. Right after that, when we'd been drinking some, she asked me, oh so casually, where I'd raised the money to buy my Graham Paige franchise. I told her we'd come into money from a relative of Lorna's and that I'd managed to borrow the rest. She said that was certainly lucky. She seemed to remember hearing we were having tough times just before that and I said yes, it was all the result of prayer. I was pretty sure she didn't believe me but there was no hate in that girl's eyes. She smiled at me and I felt she was telling me she understood and it was all okay."

I stared at him and shook my head. "You must really

be the most lovable bastard on earth, if you aren't the biggest liar."

"I'm telling you the truth, Carl. Katie was a special girl."

"Not like her ma, huh?"

"She was not one bit like Ellie, not any damn bit—"

He was so excited I could believe he'd start pounding on me if I argued, so I said, "Okay, she wasn't like Ellie." When he'd calmed down, I said, "Tell me how she was different."

"Every way. She was darker. That comes from my mother's side—black Irish—and she was lots smarter and more honest and not a whoring, teasing bitch."

"It sounds like you should have kidnapped Ellie instead of Kate. I'd guess you both would have enjoyed chopping things off Ellie. And Timmerman might've paid quicker for her."

"No, that would've been lots harder and more complicated."

"But you thought about it?"

"Never."

"Because you knew Lorna'd kill her, right?"

He shook his head but wouldn't look at me, and suddenly it was obvious he was too pooped to care whether I believed him or not. With a deep sigh he leaned back, slipped to the side against the door and gazed out the window.

"Where'd you meet Baltz?" I asked.

"He was a bootlegger for friends of ours."

"So you knew he worked out of Minneapolis and hired him to knock off the private eye, Gyles."

"Lorna did it, you were right. I was never involved. He just talked to her, I wouldn't have anything to do with any of it."

"When Kate was murdered, you knew he'd done it, didn't you?"

"I didn't *know* it. I don't *know* it now."

"You know it, sure as you're sitting here with me."

He shook his head wearily.

"It's the same as if you did it yourself," I told him. "You laid your old boss's wife, mutilated your own kid and finally let her be killed—"

"I didn't!" he yelled, turning from the window and shoving his fat red face at me. "I never did! It was Lorna—she was the one—she drove Ellie to death, made me kidnap and hurt Katie. She drove and drove me—to punish me for cheating on her—"

"So if she's such a bitch on wheels, why'd you stick with her?"

He fell back, waved his soft hands and sobbed.

"It's nothing a man like you could understand. . . . Of course, it was really all my own fault. Mine and Ellie's. I'm weak, you know. I tried to be a nice guy and not hurt anybody and that way you just wind up hurting everybody. In this world what you have to do is choose who you're not going to hurt and the hell with everybody else. When you're in love with everybody you make them all vulnerable."

He was about boring me to death, but I let him run on for a while, thinking he might get carried away enough to give something useful away. But he didn't. Pretty soon he was silent and sneaking peeks at me, trying to figure out how I'd taken it all. I kept smoking and let him stew.

Finally he sat up, arched his back, lifted his chin and placed his fingers behind his neck.

"I better get back to the cabin. Lorna's going to be worrying."

"You think this is the end of it?"

He gave me his tragic eyes, lowered his arms and leaned back.

"No, there's never going to be an end to it for me. But you got what you wanted. Tell Lieutenant Baker what happened in Minneapolis and they can work out their own theories on why Baltz killed Kate. He probably got mad because she bought her booze from that old man and he got into a quarrel with her and killed her because she threatened to call the cops. She was friends with Baker, wasn't she?"

"So why'd Baltz kill Gyles!"

"Because he was a private eye working for Kate. Look, Baker'll be tickled to death to pin the killings on a real big-city hoodlum. He'll never try to convict a little old local boy when he's got that kind of choice. Go talk to him, you'll see."

"Don't worry, I'm going to talk to him."

"But don't try to bring me into it. Or Lorna. You can't prove a thing. You'd only muddy the waters. You got no reason to want revenge on us. Katie wasn't anything to you—"

"I'm supposed to forget you tried to set me up for a murder in Minneapolis?"

"You came out fine, didn't you? You found Baltz and the police have him in jail, so you get your friend free and you even got paid for it."

"Yeah. You paid to get me out of town and let Baltz know when I was coming so he could meet the train and follow."

"I had to protect myself, didn't I? Be fair, what else could I have done?"

"I guess, being the loveable kind of guy you are, that's how it had to be. And me, being the kind of guy I am, won't let you get away with it. Now get your moldy ass out of my truck."

He stared at me with his mouth open.

I reached past him, opened the door and put my hand on his shoulder.

"Out."

"But we must be five miles from town. How'm I going to get back? What're you going to do?"

"You can walk, crawl or fly, but probably you'll flag a ride. Whatever, I won't worry about it. All I know is you've gone as far as you're going with me."

"But, Carl—" he began to plead.

I really wished he'd pull a gun or show guts enough to fight. He was heavy enough to give me trouble if he worked at it, but instead he crumpled into a whimpering heap. I glared at him, considered planting my foot on his hip and sending him to the dirt with a good shove, but kicking a cringing dog doesn't do anything but make me sick so I reached past his blubbering carcass, slammed the door, started the damned truck and took him back to his one true love.

Before we'd gone a mile he'd straightened up, blown his nose and combed his hair. Looking straight ahead, he began to talk.

"You can't know what Lorna's been through. She was never a pretty girl—had old parents—grew up on a farm with no kids to play with. When I met her at a cousin's wedding she was shy as a mouse. I'd been drinking, just a little—it was legal then—and I saw her all alone in a corner and started talking to her and in no time she was glowing. I'd been with lots of girls, never had any trouble that way, but nobody before changed in front of my eyes the way she did. When the reception was over and I was leaving she put her hand on my arm and said to me, 'Sigfried, you're the nicest, most beautiful man I've ever met.'

"I never forgot that. We got married six months later. There wasn't anything nice she wouldn't do for me. I felt like worshipped. She was never much in bed—affectionate, that's all, a good girl. Probably not anything like you've ever known, Carl."

I sure as hell hoped not.

"And then all this other business came up and she had two dead babies and everything died, except I remembered how it'd been and knew nothing was her fault—"

If I'd had any sense I'd have been listening for violins and thinking how I'd lay it on Lorna when we got to the cabin about how old sweet Sig had laid the whole kidnapping and killing in her tragic lap, but at the moment he had me feeling so sorry for her I didn't have the balls to pitch into her.

By the time we reached Kate's cabin all I wanted was his ass out so I could go somewhere for a good swig of booze with healthy people.

Sig turned to show me his wet blue eyes when I stopped the truck.

"You don't know what she's been through," he said.

"Yeah, but just think, she's had you all through it."

He gave me a kicked dog look, opened the door, climbed down and turned to face me.

"Leave us out of it, Carl. You got what you wanted. Leave us something."

With that he shut the door and headed back to Lorna.

Chapter XXIV

It was late afternoon when I called Howie. We hadn't talked since our first visit to Boswell's cell. I figured he'd be happy about the neglect so it came as a surprise when he sounded glad to hear from me.

"Hey, I hear you've been busy."

"Yeah? Who from?"

"Lieutenant Baker. He told me about your trip to Minneapolis when he called to say he was releasing Boswell. You've really impressed him, you know that?"

"Good. Look, I want to talk to you. You gonna be around for a while?"

His delight faded at the notion he might not be through with me after all.

"Well, it's pretty late in the day. How much time do you want? It shouldn't be much—Baker told me the whole story."

"I don't want to see you to brag. I got a problem and I need a lawyer's opinion."

"Well, Carl, I hate to say it, but—"

"I'll pay you for half an hour's goddamned time, okay?"

"Where'd you get the money?"

"Sig French hired me to do a job for him. I haven't

222

used up my first advance yet."

That made everything peachy. He said come on over.

When I walked in, Howie looked up from behind a desk that was nearly wall to wall, and black law books loomed behind him, clear to the ceiling. The windowless room wasn't much bigger than a walk-in closet. The only light came from a gooseneck lamp on his left.

"You'd ought to be wearing a tiger skin," I said.

"Huh?"

"You look like you're in a cave. How come a lawyer can't afford an office with a window?"

"Because I'm a new lawyer and my clients don't pay much. What do you want to talk about?"

I sat down on an unpadded wooden chair in front of his desk, leaned back and laid out Sig's story in about five minutes.

At the end he said "So?"

"You don't guess it'd make a court case?"

"You couldn't get an indictment. Of course, if Baker managed to confirm enough of it, that'd be different. But it's been a long time and a lot of the evidence would have to come out of Minneapolis. I suspect Baker and the police in the city would prefer to settle on Baltz as the killer and leave the motive to something nice and simple, like bootlegging problems."

"What if I worked on Lorna and got her to turn in her dream boy, or is it true a woman can't testify against her husband?"

"Absolutely. Wives and whores are out as witnesses."

"I don't see why."

"How'd you like to have your ex-wife on the stand testifying against you? How'd you do, eh?"

"I'd hang."

"Damn right. Most men would. Okay, your half hour's about up. That's five dollars. You want to go for ten?"

"Sue me," I said, and got up.

"Come on, Carl, you promised."

"You gonna bill me for Boswell?"

"I should, but I won't."

So I paid him his five and left.

Chapter XXV

Baker was drinking coffee and admiring the brick wall out his window when I ambled into his office. His blurred eyes behind the thick lenses told me nothing, but there was a tilt at the edge of his mouth which hinted he wasn't mad.

"Well," he said, "if it isn't the giant killer."

"You ever seen Baltz?"

He admitted he hadn't.

"He's no giant."

"The Minneapolis cops think he is—or was. I understand he's shrunk some. I can figure the·deal in the house with the tank lid—even if the old lady *could* have managed that—but how'd you take a gun away from him in your hotel room?"

"Smooth talk."

He shook his head, sat down and asked if I'd like a cup of coffee.

"Is it any good?"

"It's not even hot."

"Okay, I'll take it."

He went to the door, called his order to someone and came back. His mood was so good I expected him to pat me on the head, but instead he walked around and sat down.

"This really couldn't be sweeter," he told me. "There's nothing like finding the villain's a guy with a record who's been wanted by cops in three states. And even better, the bastard's from the Cities, not our territory."

"I'm glad you like the way things have gone, because I need a little help with another problem."

"Yeah?" He sounded a lot more cautious than eager.

"You remember that little business of two guys trying to bushwhack me?"

"Vaguely."

"I think I know who put them up to it, but I want to find out who they are and make sure they don't get lucky the next time."

"You mean they weren't pals of Baltz?"

"I think they were pals of Ryder."

"Ah," he said, and reached up to adjust his glasses.

"You know whether Ryder's hired any bully boys in line with his business somewhere along the way lately?"

"It seems like maybe he has. Hold on."

He strode to the door and hollered for Sergeant Wendworth. The sergeant showed up carrying two cups of coffee and started out after handing them over.

"Hold on, Sarge," said Baker. "Do you remember something about a guy named Ryder who hired some muscle in a contract hassle a while back?"

"Is he the blimp with a place on Lake Kampie?"

"Yeah, into real estate and contracting."

"Sure. He hired muscle more than once—mostly to collect gambling debts. With interest. We never pinned him, though."

"Who was the muscle?"

"Three or four guys. Mostly worked in pairs."

"You got any names?" I asked. "Like a pair, one short and wiry, the other big and built like a brick shithouse."

"Sounds like the Hanlon brothers. Ace and Eddie. Ace is the big one."

"What do you know about them?"

"A couple tough punks. We've had 'em in on assault charges half a dozen times. Their old man was a wheat farmer. Ran their tails off when they were kids, worked 'em so hard they've never done a day's work since Ace clobbered the old man for whaling Eddie about five years ago." Wendworth shook his head. "That was a case. The old man wanted Ace sent away, only he was still drunk when he tried to place charges and the judge isn't crazy about boozers, especially ones that punch out their kids."

He told me more about the judge than interested me and I pressed him to find out where these brothers might be found. He said they hung around a speakeasy named Foxy's.

"It's just across the tracks from the depot. They got barbecued beef, home brew and their own bathtub gin."

"I didn't think you guys knew about places like that," I said.

"*I* don't," said Baker, and he didn't smile.

"Well," I said, getting up, "thanks a lot."

"Hold on," said Baker, raising his hand. "What're you going to do?"

"Look up a speakeasy."

"Tonight?"

"Yeah."

"What time?"

"Why, you going to raid the joint?"

"No. I figure if you're going to do something stupid, it might work out for me. I want to nail those bastards. If you go in there and handle it nice and quiet—let them make the first move—you could get them off your back and hand them to me."

"Uh-huh. And you don't mind if their first move is my last, right?"

"Come on, Wilcox, you know you're a counter-puncher. What do you care if a couple punks take the first swing? You've tangled with the best."

"Not two at a time, and not when they had knives and guns. Slipping blades and bullets is a tad risky."

"They aren't going to plug you in Foxy's. They'll just tail you out of there and then make their move. The sergeant here'll cover you with a partner."

I glanced at Wendworth who looked sorrowful.

I shook my head. "You want me to go into this joint, have a belt, wave at these monkeys and walk out. They tail me, use their hardware and zing—your boys close in, nailing them red-handed. Only they're red-handed with my juice. I don't like it."

"So what the hell're you going to do? Walk into Foxy's, wade into these guys and waltz out?"

"You let the sergeant tail me and you'll find out, okay?"

"Suit yourself. We'll cover the place. If you start a riot you'll wind up in the bullpen with those two guys, and it'll be like putting two scorpions in a bottle—only in this case it'll be three."

Chapter XXVI

The night sky was clear as a Catholic's conscience after confession when I cut across the railroad tracks to Foxy's. Stars were brighter than a farmer's spring hopes and thick as grasshoppers in August. Foxy's front door was permanently locked and unlit; the operating entry was around on the west alley side.

It was no surprise to recognize the doorman as a former cellmate from the Aquatown jail. Off and on I've met lots of guys from jails in speakeasies. I remembered that this one had been called Balls. I never knew why and I didn't care to ask.

He let me into a vestibule smaller than a cell in solitary and showed me his brown teeth in a grin.

"Well, I'll be goddamned, if it ain't Carl Wilcox. How long you been out of stir?"

"Years," I lied. "I see they haven't caught up with you yet."

"Never will," he assured me. "This is a sure thing. All I got to worry about is repeal."

I looked over his shoulder and saw the north end of a bar that ran along the east wall and out of sight in the darkness beyond. It looked like at least two men were working it.

"Roosevelt'll never sign repeal," said Balls. "The little old ladies'd lynch him and he knows it. That's campaign talk."

I edged past him and stopped in the doorway. It was too dark to see much at first—just a big open room with its center full of tables and booths all along the west side. Being a week night there wasn't much action at the tables, but the bar and booths were pretty well occupied.

"You lookin' for somebody special?" asked Balls. He was so close his sleeve touched mine.

"Yeah, I was planning to meet Garbo here."

"Never heard of him."

"How about the Hanlon brothers. They around?"

"Who?"

I moved a step away and looked at him. "Don't tell me you never heard of the Hanlon brothers."

"Oh, *Hanlon*. I thought you said Scanlon. Sure, I know them. They ain't been around lately. I hear Eddie was in a accident a while back. Ace took him to Chicago where he knows a tooth-tinker—the accident busted Eddie's front teeth."

I nodded and moved further into the room, breathing in the smell of beer, squinting through the smoke and gloom. Speakeasies in our territory never had much light, not for romance but to hide how crummy the joints were.

"You want a beer?" asked Balls. "A meal, maybe a shot of moon? We got the best west of Chicago, that's a fact. You'd ought to try our barbecue—the sauce'll take all the scum off your teeth."

"I can see it worked on yours. I'm just going to have a beer and the bartender can handle that. Why don't you paddle back to your door before the revenuers bust in?"

He looked uncertain, then grinned, waved and went back.

The bartender looked some like Primo Carnera, only not so pretty, and popped a beer cap without looking at the bottle while he watched me. I saw the foam rise to the top, and a few drops spilled over. He shoved the bottle across the smooth bar top and said that'd be fifteen cents. The tone dared me to bitch. I shelled out as if I always paid three times what a brew was worth and took a healthy swig. It was fairly cold and not watered an awful lot. The bartender turned his attention to another customer and I looked back to see what Balls was up to.

He was in conference with a gray-suited bruiser almost as big as the bartender and they were both looking at me. I lifted my bottle in salute. Balls grinned weakly, the bruiser scowled. A moment later he was leaning against the bar to my right.

"The beer's a mite strong on water," I told him.

"That's too bad. Maybe you'd better find a place where they make it stronger."

"You know a place?"

"This is the only joint I know in Aquatown."

"I'd think you'd want to keep track of the competition."

"We haven't got any. We run a nice quiet place and nobody's died from our moon and nobody fights here. When you get through with your beer, just move on out. When you get outside, keep walking. Okay?"

"What's the matter? You figure I'm a revenuer?"

"I know exactly who and what you are, Wilcox. And

you're not going to start anything in here. You want to settle something, go someplace else."

His nose was flatter than mine, he'd fought often and lost his share, but I guessed he'd won his share too. He was big, wide, strong and mean. An ideal bouncer, the kind that almost never has to use his muscle. One look turns even drunk punks tame.

"Are the Hanlons friends of yours?"

"My only friend runs this joint. He says there's gonna be no trouble here. That's how it is."

"I don't figure on starting trouble."

"Don't try to shit me," he said in a very pleasant voice. "Just you being here is going to start trouble if the right guys show and you goddamn know it. Now drink your beer and go your way."

I liked his style. Another night, when I was five years younger and didn't have a program, I'd sure as hell have invited him to remove me if he felt up to it. Now I thought that even if I could chop him down to my size, it'd take time, and sure as hell the other heavies around the place wouldn't stand by admiring my talent. It could be a little worse than embarrassing to find myself pitched out in the street in front of the Hanlon boys in something short of my best shape for a waltz.

I took another swig of beer and looked the bouncer over, top to bottom.

"You must be as big as Lieutenant Baker," I said.

His head drew back half an inch. "You know the lieutenant?"

"He knows I'm here."

He thought that over. "You got a gun?"

I stood, raised my elbows and let him check me out.

"All right. When they come," he said, "don't make a move toward them. When you leave, do it fast and careful. Nothing's going to happen in here. You got that?"

"Sure. You gonna tell them?"

The bartender had just poured my third beer when the side door opened and I caught sight of the Hanlon brothers pushing past Balls. As far as I could tell he didn't speak to them and they ignored him. I turned on my stool and watched them walk through the door, turn to their left and head for the booths along the west wall.

Ace wasn't as tall as the bouncer, but he was just as wide and a lot younger. He had a neck thick as old oak and his head tapered up from massive jaws to a narrow crown covered with strawish hair. Eddie, small and smooth as a shadow, had a piece of tape across his upper lip that looked like a lopsided white mustache in the dim light. Eddie's eyes darted all over the place, but passed so quickly I didn't think he spotted me. The moment they were seated in the third booth from the back, Eddie leaned forward and then Ace slowly turned to stare my way.

A waiter took drinks to their table automatically—a shot for Eddie, a beer for Ace. Eddie downed the shot with two quick gulps, slipped out of the booth and strolled through the room, past Balls and into the alley.

That was about the only move I hadn't expected and it bothered me. Was he going after reinforcements or had he left his artillery behind and set off to remedy the shortage? The bouncer was bothered too and drifted over to Ace's booth. Their exchange told me that the bouncer hadn't lied when he told me he wasn't palsy with the Hanlons. Ace answered when spoken to but never looked at the man, and his attitude was that of a snooker player being questioned by a kibitzer when he was lining up a tough shot.

I stood and started working my way through the tables toward the booth. The bouncer caught my movement out of the corner of his eye and turned to scowl. Ace's small eyes watched without expression.

"You going to frisk him?" I asked the bouncer.

"Go back to the bar," he ordered.

A couple chairs scraped behind me and I turned to see four guys scramble from a table and head east. I turned back to Ace. His hands were wrapped around his bottle and his eyes were steady on mine. Slowly he grinned.

"Sit down, Wilcox," he said.

The bouncer hesitated as I slipped into the seat Eddie had left. Ace looked at the bouncer. "Tell Tommy to bring Wilcox a beer, okay?"

The bouncer gave him a long, flat stare, then walked back to the bar.

Ace swigged his beer, wiped his mouth and leaned against the booth back.

"I got used to you as a rabbit," he said. "How come all of a sudden you're a bloodhound?"

"I didn't have time to mess with you before. And, besides, you always showed up with hardware."

He kept grinning at me as if he were all full of happy.

"You doubled back in the cornfield, didn't you?"

I nodded. "You passed me two rows away. If you'd come one closer we'd have settled everything right then."

His grin faded a little. "You couldn't take me. Not in a million years."

I turned, leaned against the wall and put my right foot on the bench beside me. A waiter delivered my beer. He didn't look at either of us and I guessed he planned to tell the truth when he was questioned later—he'd say he never looked at faces, only tips.

The bouncer watched us in the bar mirror.

I sipped the beer and wondered just how crazy this Hanlon might be. His eyes reminded me of men I'd known in the army and prison; the ones everybody admired because, as they always said, old so-and-so don't give a shit for nothing. These were the real madmen who never thought a second about the day, or even hour, to come. These are men who only know now.

Ace dropped his hands in his lap. I turned to square with him and planted both feet tight under the bench while I watched his shoulders and tried to remember if he'd done anything on the rock that night on the beach which would tell me if he was right or lefthanded. He drank with his right, but that's a nice way to hide a lefthanded draw.

"Where'd Eddie go?" I asked.

"I sent him home. When we tried to talk with you on the beach you split his lip and busted three teeth. Another kick in the mouth might be bad for him."

"You think another kick in the head's going to help you?"

"The nice thing about a booth," he told me, "is that a guy can't kick you from one. Not in the head."

"You care to bet on that?"

He grinned so wide I could see his brown gums and a molar gap.

"I just might."

I laughed, leaned back and pulled my beer bottle into my lap below the table edge. "You remind me of a gambler con I knew at Stillwater. He told me, 'Son, don't never take another man's bet. I don't care if he offers you odds the Queen of Hearts is gonna piss in your ear. Don't bet she won't 'cause sure as sunrise if you do, your eardrums gonna soak in salty hot.' "

Ace showed me his gums and tooth gap again, but his eyes flicked toward the kitchen door a few yards behind me and to my left. I shifted my grip on the almost-full beer bottle, so I was holding it for a club swing. Then Ace's right shoulder dropped and the bouncer yelled, "Look out, Wilcox!"

I came to my feet, jerked the table loose with my left hand and rammed the far edge into Ace's middle as I swung the beer bottle overhand and brought it down on his thick skull. As the bottle exploded I heard two shots, one under the table, the other from a ways behind, both deafening. Nothing hit me. Ace slumped, swung his head in a short arc and slowly gripped the table edge with hammy hands. I glimpsed a struggle by the kitchen door when I turned my head. Ace began to rise, clutching the table edge. I slipped from the booth, reached back, grabbed his straw hair and jerked him clear of the table. I wheeled him around and gave him a boot in the ass that shot him into the center tables, scrabbling on his hands and knees while his bullet head scattered furniture like a cannon ball.

Before I could follow him up about three guys came between us, and a fourth grabbed my arm.

"Okay, okay," said Sergeant Wendworth. "You made your point, Wilcox, just take it easy."

Chapter XXVII

"What'd Lieutenant Baker say when you went back to the station?" asked Avril as we walked Lake Kampie's beach the next morning.

"He said I was an idiot and a lot of other things."

"He should have been grateful. Didn't he tell you he wanted to arrest those two?"

"He didn't like getting furniture smashed up when he had his men spotted in an illegal joint."

Actually he wasn't too sore and he told me I must be tougher than old moose shit. He couldn't see how I managed, being such a half-pint.

"Well," said Avril, "he's right about you being an idiot. What in the world did you think you were going to do, walking into that place and taking on those two maniacs alone?"

"I never figured on being alone. That's why I went and talked with Baker. I knew he'd have me covered."

"It was still crazy."

"Not really. I figured on surprising them. It didn't seem likely they'd carry hardware when they just went out for a drink and I couldn't imagine a guy as big as Ace thinking he needed a rod on him all the time. One of those damned things is heavy enough to pull a man's britches off if he sticks it in his pocket. What I did worry about was Eddie's knife. That's why, when he drifted out, I decided to join Ace. I wanted to crowd him into doing something stupid."

"My God, I don't see how you've lived into middle age taking chances like that."

"I'm not middle-aged. I'm just in my advanced youth."

She hugged my arm and laughed when we bumped hips and lost stride. "Come on, Carl, what do you want to be when you grow up?"

"Tall."

"You're tall enough, silly."

"Enough's never enough. What I want is more. I wish it were dark."

"You're very tall in the dark," she assured me.

"It helps, but that's not why I want it dark now."

"Well, how about we take a ride. Maybe we can find some deep shade somewhere. . . ."

We found dandy shade in Ole Johanson's grove and made the best use of it for over an hour. After her sleep, Avril woke, stretched and took a walk with me.

"We're going to have to find a better place for loving than that blamed truck," she said. "I keep getting kinks."

"Have you left Ryder for good?"

"Of course."

"Okay, don't snap at me just because now you've had what you wanted."

She laughed, cuffed my arm and then turned sober.

"Listen, I don't really want to hear any more about him, okay? It was a dumb thing, living with him at all. It was idiotic to keep it up after we weren't friends anymore, and I hate even thinking about him, so lay off—please?"

"Where're you going to live?"

"I'll share with a girlfriend in town."

"It's too bad you can't buy a cabin on the lake. Maybe you could rent one."

"Sure, and I'll buy a new Buick to drive back and forth to work in town. What could be simpler?"

"What we can do," I said, "is talk to a couple people who're trying to unload a cabin and get out of state."

She halted and looked at me as I turned to face her.

"You mean Kate's place. You want to talk to the Frenches again."

"Well, it wouldn't hurt, would it?"

"Jesus Christ," she said, and began walking once more. I went along. "You really have a one-track mind, don't you? Have you ever stopped thinking about that murder?"

"Lots of times. Always when you turned warm."

"Uh-huh. Well, I'm all warmed out. And above all, I don't want any damned thing to do with the Frenches. You go do what you have to, just leave me out, okay?"

It was a little after four P.M. when I wheeled into the drive behind Kate's cabin and parked. Sig's car was missing and for a second I was sure they'd flown the coop. Then Lorna's face appeared in the kitchen window. It took a moment before I recognized her; black hair curtained her cheeks and made waves over her shoulders, somehow blunting the sharp nose and softening her sharp chin. She disappeared from the window and showed up in the back doorway as I walked across the dry grass to meet her.

"You've just washed your hair," I said.

Her right hand came up and touched the dark mass at her cheek. Instead of the usual expression of sullenness or anger, her face had a melancholy, almost dreamy look.

I halted at the stoop.

"You'd ought to wear it like that all the time, it looks great."

"It's less trouble up," she said.

"It's worth trouble the way you've got it. Can we talk a little?"

Her eyes became more alert. "What about?"

"How about you?"

"Me?" Now she was wary.

"Yeah. I've talked a lot with Sig. He's told me lots about himself and some of you, but he's such a born liar I thought maybe I could get a straighter story from you."

"When did you talk with Sig?" she demanded.

"Day before yesterday. Didn't you know? Where'd he tell you he was going?"

She dropped her eyes, thought a moment and shrugged.

"I thought he was going to see Kate's lawyer."

"So you didn't know he spent the morning talking with me about what really happened to Kate's hand when she was a little girl?"

She lifted her head and peered at me through her lashes.

"I think you're trying to be clever."

"Yeah, I'm not too good at it, am I? How about you invite me in and we talk this whole business over? You've got nothing to worry about since you know I can't outsmart you."

"Oh, no, mister," she said, shaking her head hard enough to make her hair toss. "You're not getting me alone in the house."

That about stunned me for a moment. She actually believed if I got her alone my first move would be to grab her and drag her into the bedroom. She probably thought I couldn't even get that far before my lust made me ravish her on the living room carpet.

When it comes to thinking about rape, you can't hardly beat sexless folks and puritans.

"Well," I said, "how about we go out there on the beach in front of God and everybody, and just talk? That'd be safe now, wouldn't it?"

She thought that over while watching me suspiciously and finally said all right, she'd bring a chair. She didn't offer to bring two.

So a few minutes later, there we were, sitting under the sun on the broad beach before the cabin. Lorna perched on a folding chair which sank two inches into the dry sand before it steadied. I sat, tailor fashion, half-facing her and the lake.

"What'd Sig tell you I told him about Minneapolis?" I asked.

"He said nothing happened. You talked to some people there, including the police, and came up with nothing."

"He didn't tell you what happened to Baltz?"

Her head jerked. "Who?"

"Baltz. Sig's bootlegger friend who kills people now and then."

"My husband has no bootlegger friends."

"All right, so he was an acquaintance, or maybe a business associate. Whatever, he killed a private eye that Kate had hired to find who her real father was and

he was supposed to kill me, too, only it didn't take. Now
he's in the Minneapolis jail, probably singing like my
old man's canary."

She sniffed and said, "Really?" She wouldn't have
been less worried if I'd threatened her with a thunder-
bolt out of the clear sky above.

"Okay," I said, giving her my rueful, what-the-hell
grin. "So I can't touch you two. But the story he gives
me is such a great one I've just got to hear your version.
Nobody can hear you but me and nobody'd believe either one of us anyway if what Sig said is even close to the
truth, but I'm busting to know and if you unload maybe
I'll be able to settle for just that and give the whole
thing up."

She didn't bother accusing me of trying to be clever
this time, she just gave me a Mona Lisa smile.

I gave up being sweet. "Sig tells me the kidnapping
was your idea. So was the mutilation and the ransom
amount. He says you wanted revenge because Ellie seduced him and ruined your life. He says you made him
chop off Kate's fingers to prove that you meant more to
him than Ellie or that kid, and he did it to atone. Has he
got all of that right?"

The statements hit her like punches in combinations,
her head jerked and her eyes glazed.

"Was it that way?" I pressed.

"You're lying," she whispered. Then her eyes became wide and bright as she leaned toward me. "Liar!"
she shrieked.

She scrambled to her feet so quickly the chair tilted
back and stood on two buried legs as she scrambled over
the beach, across the lawn and around the cabin.

I watched her go, then got to my feet, pulled the
chair from the sand and carried it to the back stoop

where I left it. Before I got to my truck, Sig drove up in Kate's black Buick. I leaned against the truck hood and watched Sig open the car door and slip out. His face was haggard.

"What the hell are you doing here?" he demanded.

"Just had a little chat with Lorna."

"You've no business sneaking around, talking to a man's wife behind his back."

"It's always better talking to a man's wife behind his back. But don't worry. Lorna doesn't like talking as much as you do. She listened real good, though. I can see why you two get along so great. What'd you learn from Kate's attorney?"

"That's none of your goddamned business. What'd you tell Lorna?"

"Nothing she didn't know. Only what you told me. I figured I'd ought to know her view of things. . . ."

His heavy face sagged. He licked his lips, worked his mouth and looked toward the house with fear. He gave a tragic sigh and began walking toward the house with brimming eyes.

When I walked into the police station a while later, Sergeant Wendworth said Baker had been looking for me.

"Trot back and see him. He's really jumping."

The moment I walked in his door Baker asked where the hell I'd been.

"At Kate's cabin, talking to Lorna French."

He got up, walked around and sat down on the corner of his desk. "All right," he said, taking off his glasses so I could see he was glaring. "Who hired Baltz to kill Kate?"

"Don't you know?" I didn't bother to try looking innocent since I knew he couldn't see me without his glasses. He put them back on.

"Yeah, I know. But I want to know if you do and if you can prove it."

"I thought you were all happy with having a foreigner taking the rap."

"Never mind giving me a lot of shit. What happened in Minneapolis? What'd you find out? I want the whole goddamned story. The one you should've told me when you came back."

"I didn't want to spoil your happiness—"

"What you wanted was a couple babysitters to get the Hanlons off your ass and that's all you talked about. You caught me in a good mood and suckered me into doing your goddamned laundry."

So I started talking and all the while wondered what suddenly made it important to him. It had to be something about the will. She must have anticipated the murder.

Baker kept at me for nearly two hours, even brought in a stenographer and had her take notes on a shorthand pad.

"As soon as I found out the guy in the gray suit was Baltz, I figured he was the guy who strangled Kate. He was familiar with our territory, he was a born killer and he could never resist stealing booze. He highjacked it from the mob and he stole it from Kate's cabin and Boswell's truck because it was there. I don't believe he ever even saw Boswell there on the couch, and I doubt if he'd dream anybody'd be dumb enough to think that old guy could strangle anybody. Baltz isn't tricky. He's an action guy."

"How about when he came to your room at the hotel? Why didn't he just knock you off?"

"He wanted to know if I'd learned anything important and maybe passed it on to somebody else."

"And you look so sad-assed he figured you were harmless and got careless. He didn't have a notion about what a tough bastard you are."

"I'm not tough. Just a little sudden now and then."

"And lucky. Jesus. Okay, where's Avril now? I want to talk to her."

Two days later they read the will. Since I wasn't one of the lucky gang mentioned I wasn't invited, but Avril told me the story.

Kate left the cabin and five thousand dollars cash to Avril with a few choice remarks about how it would free her from servitude to Ryder. Polly, the red-haired neighbor girl, got two thousand dollars to be turned over on her twenty-first birthday and spent for whatever she pleased. The house in town went to Frances (Fancy) Franklin, "because she is beautiful and talented and will probably never land for long but should have a place of her own to come back to when her career ends."

She left five hundred dollars to Boswell because he was "kind and gentle and, most of all, competent." He made the "best moonshine in South Dakota."

"If I die suddenly," she concluded, "however it happens, murder should be expected. And if it is murder, I leave the Buick to the person responsible for bringing the murderer, or murderers, to justice. In view of his talents and personal interest, I would expect this to be Lieutenant Baker and the automobile should be the added incentive necessary to avenge me. After my murderer, or murderers, have been apprehended, if my kind cousin, Sig, and his wife, Lorna, are still at liberty, I leave all of my remaining cash assets to them. If they are indicted for my murder, none of my money should go to them to pay for their defense and if they are convicted the assets will be turned over to the following charities . . .

MORE MYSTERIOUS PLEASURES

HAROLD ADAMS
The Carl Wilcox mystery series
MURDER	#501	$3.95
PAINT THE TOWN RED	#601	$3.95
THE MISSING MOON	#602	$3.95
THE NAKED LIAR	#420	$3.95
THE FOURTH WIDOW	#502	$3.50
THE BARBED WIRE NOOSE	#603	$3.95

TED ALLBEURY
THE SEEDS OF TREASON	#604	$3.95

ERIC AMBLER
HERE LIES: AN AUTOBIOGRAPHY	#701	$8.95

ROBERT BARNARD
A TALENT TO DECEIVE: AN APPRECIATION OF AGATHA CHRISTIE	#702	$8.95

EARL DERR BIGGERS
The Charlie Chan mystery series
THE HOUSE WITHOUT A KEY	#421	$3.95
THE CHINESE PARROT	#503	$3.95
BEHIND THAT CURTAIN	#504	$3.95
THE BLACK CAMEL	#505	$3.95
CHARLIE CHAN CARRIES ON	#506	$3.95
KEEPER OF THE KEYS	#605	$3.95

JAMES M. CAIN
THE ENCHANTED ISLE	#415	$3.95
CLOUD NINE	#507	$3.95

ROBERT CAMPBELL
IN LA-LA LAND WE TRUST	#508	$3.95

RAYMOND CHANDLER
RAYMOND CHANDLER'S UNKNOWN THRILLER:
   THE SCREENPLAY OF "PLAYBACK"   #703 $9.95

GEORGE C. CHESBRO
The Veil Kendry suspense series
VEIL   #509 $3.95
JUNGLE OF STEEL AND STONE   #606 $3.95

MATTHEW HEALD COOPER
DOG EATS DOG   #607 $4.95

CARROLL JOHN DALY
THE ADVENTURES OF SATAN HALL   #704 $8.95

NORBERT DAVIS
THE ADVENTURES OF MAX LATIN   #705 $8.95

WILLIAM L. DeANDREA
The Cronus espionage series
SNARK   #510 $3.95
AZRAEL   #608 $4.50
The Matt Cobb mystery series
KILLED IN THE ACT   #511 $3.50
KILLED WITH A PASSION   #512 $3.50
KILLED ON THE ICE   #513 $3.50

LEN DEIGHTON
ONLY WHEN I LAUGH   #609 $4.95

AARON ELKINS
The Professor Gideon Oliver mystery series
OLD BONES   #610 $3.95

JAMES ELLROY
THE BLACK DAHLIA   #611 $4.95
SUICIDE HILL   #514 $3.95

PAUL ENGLEMAN
The Mark Renzler mystery series
CATCH A FALLEN ANGEL   #515 $3.50
MURDER-IN-LAW   #612 $3.95

LOREN D. ESTLEMAN
The Peter Macklin suspense series
ROSES ARE DEAD   #516 $3.95
ANY MAN'S DEATH   #517 $3.95

ANNE FINE
THE KILLJOY #613 $3.95

DICK FRANCIS
THE SPORT OF QUEENS #410 $3.95

JOHN GARDNER
THE GARDEN OF WEAPONS #103 $4.50

BRIAN GARFIELD
DEATH WISH #301 $3.95
DEATH SENTENCE #302 $3.95
TRIPWIRE #303 $3.95
FEAR IN A HANDFUL OF DUST #304 $3.95

THOMAS GODFREY, ED.
MURDER FOR CHRISTMAS #614 $3.95
MURDER FOR CHRISTMAS II #615 $3.95

JOE GORES
COME MORNING #518 $3.95

JOSEPH HANSEN
The Dave Brandstetter mystery series
EARLY GRAVES #643 $3.95

NAT HENTOFF
THE MAN FROM INTERNAL AFFAIRS #409 $3.95

PATRICIA HIGHSMITH
THE ANIMAL-LOVER'S BOOK
OF BEASTLY MURDER #706 $8.95
LITTLE TALES OF MISOGYNY #707 $8.95
SLOWLY, SLOWLY IN THE WIND #708 $8.95

DOUG HORNIG
WATERMAN #616 $3.95
The Loren Swift mystery series
THE DARK SIDE #519 $3.95

JANE HORNING
THE MYSTERY LOVERS' BOOK
OF QUOTATIONS #709 $9.95

P.D. JAMES/T.A. CRITCHLEY
THE MAUL AND THE PEAR TREE #520 $3.95

STUART M. KAMINSKY
The Toby Peters mystery series

HE DONE HER WRONG	#105	$3.95
HIGH MIDNIGHT	#106	$3.95
NEVER CROSS A VAMPIRE	#107	$3.95
BULLET FOR A STAR	#308	$3.95
THE FALA FACTOR	#309	$3.95

JOSEPH KOENIG

FLOATER	#521	$3.50

ELMORE LEONARD

THE HUNTED	#401	$3.95
MR. MAJESTYK	#402	$3.95
THE BIG BOUNCE	#403	$3.95

ELSA LEWIN

I, ANNA	#522	$3.50

PETER LOVESEY

ROUGH CIDER	#617	$3.95
BUTCHERS AND OTHER STORIES OF CRIME	#710	$9.95

ARTHUR LYONS
The Jacob Asch mystery series

FAST FADE	#618	$3.95

ED McBAIN

ANOTHER PART OF THE CITY	#524	$3.95

The Matthew Hope mystery series

SNOW WHITE AND ROSE RED	#414	$3.95
CINDERELLA	#525	$3.95
PUSS IN BOOTS	#629	$3.95

VINCENT McCONNOR

LIMBO	#630	$3.95

GREGORY MCDONALD, ED.

LAST LAUGHS: THE 1986 MYSTERY WRITERS OF AMERICA ANTHOLOGY	#711	$8.95

CHARLOTTE MacLEOD
The Professor Peter Shandy mystery series

THE CORPSE IN OOZAK'S POND	#627	$3.95

WILLIAM MARSHALL
The Yellowthread Street mystery series

YELLOWTHREAD STREET	#619	$3.50
THE HATCHET MAN	#620	$3.50
GELIGNITE	#621	$3.50
THIN AIR	#622	$3.95
THE FAR AWAY MAN	#623	$3.50
ROADSHOW	#624	$3.95
HEAD FIRST	#625	$3.50
FROGMOUTH	#626	$3.50

THOMAS MAXWELL

KISS ME ONCE	#523	$4.95
THE SABERDENE VARIATIONS	#628	$4.95

FREDERICK NEBEL

THE ADVENTURES OF CARDIGAN	#712	$9.95

WILLIAM F. NOLAN

THE BLACK MASK BOYS: MASTERS IN THE HARD-BOILED SCHOOL OF DETECTIVE FICTION	#713	$8.95

PETER O'DONNELL
The Modesty Blaise suspense series

DEAD MAN'S HANDLE	#526	$3.95

ELIZABETH PETERS
The Amelia Peabody mystery series

CROCODILE ON THE SANDBANK	#209	$3.95
THE CURSE OF THE PHARAOHS	#210	$3.95

The Jacqueline Kirby mystery series

THE SEVENTH SINNER	#411	$3.95
THE MURDERS OF RICHARD III	#412	$3.95

ANTHONY PRICE
The Doctor David Audley espionage series

THE LABYRINTH MAKERS	#404	$3.95
THE ALAMUT AMBUSH	#405	$3.95
COLONEL BUTLER'S WOLF	#527	$3.95
OCTOBER MEN	#529	$3.95
OTHER PATHS TO GLORY	#530	$3.95
OUR MAN IN CAMELOT	#631	$3.95
WAR GAME	#632	$4.95
THE '44 VINTAGE	#633	$3.95
TOMORROW'S GHOST	#634	$3.95
SION CROSSING	#406	$3.95
HERE BE MONSTERS	#528	$3.95
FOR THE GOOD OF THE STATE	#635	$4.95

CHRIS WILTZ
The Neal Rafferty mystery series
A DIAMOND BEFORE YOU DIE   #645 $3.95

CORNELL WOOLRICH/LAWRENCE BLOCK
INTO THE NIGHT   #646 $3.95

■ ■

AVAILABLE AT YOUR BOOKSTORE OR DIRECT FROM THE PUBLISHER

Mysterious Press Mail Order
129 West 56th Street
New York, NY 10019

Please send me the MYSTERIOUS PRESS titles I have circled below:

103 105 106 107 112 113 209 210 211 212 213 214 301 302
303 304 308 309 315 316 401 402 403 404 405 406 407 408
409 410 411 412 413 414 415 416 417 418 419 420 421 501
502 503 504 505 506 507 508 509 510 511 512 513 514 515
516 517 518 519 520 521 522 523 524 525 526 527 528 529
530 531 532 533 534 535 536 537 538 539 540 541 542 543
544 545 601 602 603 604 605 606 607 608 609 610 611 612
613 614 615 616 617 618 619 620 621 622 623 624 625 626
627 628 629 630 631 632 633 634 635 636 637 638 639 640
641 642 643 644 645 646 701 702 703 704 705 706 707 708
709 710 711 712 713 714 715 716 717 718 719 720 721 722

I am enclosing $_____ (please add $3.00 postage and handling
for the first book, and 25¢ for each additional book). Send check or
money order only—no cash or C.O.D.'s please. Allow at least 4 weeks
for delivery.

NAME _____

ADDRESS _____

CITY _____ STATE _____ ZIP CODE _____
New York State residents please add appropriate sales tax.